THE
LAST JOY

Knut Hamsun

THE
LAST *J*OY

Translated from the Norwegian by Sverre Lyngstad

MASTERWORKS OF FICTION
(1912)

GREEN INTEGER
KØBENHAVN & LOS ANGELES
2003

GREEN INTEGER
Edited by Per Bregne
København / Los Angeles

Distributed in the United States and Canada by
Consortium Book Sales and Distribution
1045 Westgate Drive, Suite 90
Saint Paul, Minnesota 55114-1065

(323) 857-1115 / http://www.greeninteger.com

English language translation ©2003 by Sverre Lyngstad
Published originally as *Den siste Glæde* (Kristiania: Gyldendal, 1912)
Back cover material ©2003 Green Integer
All rights reserved

Cover Photograph: Knut Hamsun
Design: Per Bregne
Typography & Cover: Trudy Fisher

LIBRARY OF CONGRESS CATALOGING IN PUBLICATION DATA
Knut Hamsun [1859-1952]
The Last Joy
p. cm — Green Integer 90
ISBN: 1-931243-19-0 (alk. paper)
I. Title II. Series III. Translator

Printed in the United States of America on acid-free paper.
Green Integer Books are published for Douglas Messerli

THE
LAST *JOY*

Now I've gone into the forest.

Not that I'm sore about anything, or particularly hurt by men's wickedness; but since the forest won't come to me I have to go to it. That's the way it is.

This time I didn't set out as a slave or tramp. I'm well off and overfed, sluggish with luck and success. You understand? I abandoned the world as a sultan abandons rich food and his harem and flowers, and dons a hair shirt.

I suppose I could make more of it. For I mean to wander about here and think and make great irons red. Nietzsche would probably have said something like this: The last word I spoke, men approved, they nodded. But it was my last word, I went into the forest. For then I understood that what I had said was either dishonest or stupid. . . .

I made no such pronouncement, but simply went into the forest.

＊

Don't get the idea that nothing ever happens here. The snowflakes drift down here just as in town, and birds and beasts attend to their chores from morning till night, and from night till morning as well. I could send quite a few dark tales from here, but I won't. I've sought the forest for solitude and for the sake of my great irons; I do have some great irons in me starting to glow. So I manage myself accordingly. If I meet a reindeer buck some day, maybe I'll say, "Good heavens, there is a reindeer buck, he's fierce!" But if that makes too much of an impression on me, then I say it's a calf or a chicken, feeding myself a pack of lies.

Nothing happening here!

One day I saw two Lapps meet, a boy and a girl. At first they behaved like other people. *Boris!* they said to one another and smiled. But a moment later they fell down in the snow and I lost track of them for quite some time. You'd better check on them, I thought after a quarter of an hour had gone by, they might suffocate in the snow. Then up they came and went their separate ways.

I've never seen such a greeting in all my threadbare life.

*

I live day and night in an abandoned turf hut which I have to crawl into. Someone must have put it up long ago and used it in a pinch, maybe a hunted man holed up here for a few days in the fall. We are two of us in the hut, but if I don't count Madame as a human, I'm alone. Madame is a mouse I live with, I've given her this name to honor her. She eats anything I lay aside in the corners and sits watching me from time to time.

I graciously left to Madame the old hay that was in the hut when I first came; for my own bed I cut some soft pine sprigs, as was right and proper. I have an ax and saw and what dishes I need. And I have a sleeping bag of sheepskin with the wool on the inside. I keep the fire on the hearth burning all night, my jacket hanging nearby smells freshly of pine pitch in the morning. When I want some coffee I go out and fill the kettle with clean snow and hang it over the fire, then I'll have water.

But can this really be called life?

There you made a slip of the tongue. It's a life you can't understand. Sure, you have your home in town, and you have furnished it with knickknacks and pictures and books; but you have a wife and a maid and a hundred expenses. Waking or sleeping, you are in a race with things, never at peace. I am at peace. Keep your bright ideas and books and art and newspapers, keep your cafés too and your whiskey, which only makes me sick every time. Here I walk the forest and feel contented. If you ask me intellectual questions and try to catch me out, I merely answer, say, that

God is the source and that men are verily just dots and specks of dust in the universe. Nor have *you* gotten any further. But if you go so far as to ask me what eternity is, I've gotten exactly as far as you in this, too, and answer, Eternity is just uncreated time, simply uncreated time.

My friend, come here and I'll take a mirror from my pocket and set a spot of sunlight on your face and illuminate you, my little friend.

*

You lie in bed till ten or eleven and still feel tired and run-down when you get up. I can see you coming out into the street, your eyes squinting at a morning that has dawned too early. I get up at five, thoroughly rested. It's still dark out, but there is plenty to see all the same: the moon, the stars, the clouds and the weather omens for the day. I figure out the weather for hours ahead. In what key is that soughing in the air? Is the crack of the ice on the Glimma Lake dry and light or deep and long? My ear picks up some splendid signs, and as it grows lighter I add the visible signs to what I hear and become more and more knowledgeable.

Then a narrow strip of day appears low in the east, the stars draw back from the sky and light reigns.

Shortly a raven circles over the forest and I warn Madame not to show herself outside the hut and be gobbled up.

But if there is new snow, trees, thickets and boulders take on monstrous, unearthly shapes, as though they had come from another world in the night. A windfallen pine with its root torn up looks like a witch that got paralyzed in the midst of some weird antics.

Here a hare has leaped, there are the tracks of a lone reindeer. I take out my sleeping bag and hang it high in a tree because of Madame, who will eat anything, and follow the reindeer tracks into the forest. I can tell that it moved along quite at leisure, but with a definite goal, walking due east, into the morning. At the river Skjel, so turbulent it never freezes over, the reindeer drank, scraped the ground for moss, rested briefly and moved on.

And what this reindeer did is, maybe, all I learn and experience that day. It's something, I think. The days are short, by two o'clock when I shuffle homeward it's already full twilight and the good, still night draws on. I start cooking. I have plenty of meat in three sparkling-white snowdrifts, I even have what's better: eight fat reindeer cheeses to eat with butter and flatbread.

While the pot is boiling I lie down a bit, gaze at the fire and fall asleep. I take my nap before the meal. And when I awake the pot is ready, an aroma of meat and pitch pine fills the hut. Madame darts back and forth on the floor and eventually gets her share. I eat and light my pipe.

The day is over. It was good in every way, I had no vexations. In the great silence that surrounds me I'm the only full-grown human astir, I grow larger and more important that way, God's neighbor. And I believe the red irons within me will turn out well, for God does great things for his neighbor.

I lie and think about the reindeer, the path it took, what it did at the Skjel River and how it wandered on. There it slipped under some branches where its horns grazed the bark, leaving some marks; there an osier thicket forced it to turn aside, but just beyond the thicket it straightened out the curve and kept on going east. I think about all this.

And you? Did you read in one newspaper, as opposed to some other newspaper, what Norwegian public opinion is about Social Security right now?

II

On stormy days I sit inside and lose myself in one thing or another. I also write letters to a few friends, telling them I'm doing well and hoping to hear the same from them. But I have no way of mailing these letters and they get older and older every day. Well, no matter. I've tied the letters up with a string that hangs from the ceiling, to keep Madame from gnawing them.

Then one day a man came walking my way. He had a hasty, sliding gait; his clothes were nothing to brag about and his neck was bare, a laboring man. He was carrying a bag, whatever there might be in it. "Hello," we say to each other, "nice weather in the woods."

"I didn't expect to find any people in the hut," the man says. His manner was at once peevish and bold, he threw his bag down without ceremony.

He must know something about me, I thought, since he acts like such a big shot.

"Have you been here long?" he asks. "Will you be leaving soon?"

"Is the hut yours maybe?" I ask in return.

He gave me a hard look.

"Because if the hut is yours, that's something else,"

13

I said. "But when I leave I don't intend to take it with me, like some pickpocket."

I said it gently and playfully, not to get in trouble because of my mouth.

But I'd said exactly the right thing, the man suddenly lost his nerve. One way or another I'd made him understand that I knew more about him than he did about me.

When I invited him in he was grateful and said, "Thanks, but I'm afraid I'll just carry in snow."

Then he brushed his boots with great care, took his bag and crawled in.

"I could manage some coffee," I said.

"Don't go to any trouble," he answered, wiping his face and puffing with warmth. "I've had quite a tramp, though, all night."

"Going over the mountain, are you?"

"It depends. I don't suppose there's work to be had on the other side either now, with winter and all."

He took the coffee.

"Would you have a scrap of food? It's a shame to ask. A piece of flatbread? I didn't manage to bring anything."

"Sure, flatbread, butter and reindeer cheese. Help yourself."

"You know, it ain't so easy for lots of folks in the winter," the man said as he ate.

"Could you, by any chance, go back down to the village with some letters from me?" I ask. "You won't do it for nothing."

"No, I'm darned if I can," the man answers. "I'm afraid not. In any case, I just have to get to the other side, I've heard there's work to be had at Hillingen, in the Hilling Forest. So I really can't."

I've got to put him on his mettle again, I thought. Now he just sits there moping; he'll wind up asking me for a half krone. I put my hand on his bag and said, "What are you carrying? Heavy stuff?"

"What's it to you?" he snapped, pulling the bag away.

"I wasn't going to steal anything, I'm no thief," I said, again speaking playfully.

"I don't care what you are," he mumbled.

The day was wearing on. With a stranger around I didn't feel like going out into the woods, but preferred to chat with him and draw him out. He was an ordinary man, not much interested in my irons, with dirty hands, ignorant and tiresome in his talk; no doubt he'd stolen what was in the bag. Later I realized he was wise in many little things that life had taught him. He complained that his heels were cold and took off his boots. No wonder he was cold, there were no heels to his socks, only holes. He borrowed a knife from me and cut away the ragged parts, then pulled the socks on again backward, with the soles over his insteps. When he'd gotten his boots back on, he said, "There, now I'm nice and warm."

He was harmless. If he took the saw or ax from the corner to look it over, he put it back in its place again. When he examined the letters and maybe tried to read the addresses, he didn't let them go carelessly and leave them swinging, but took care first to steady the string. I had no reason to complain about him.

He stayed for dinner, and when he'd eaten he said, "Excuse me, but do you mind if I go and cut myself some pine twigs to sit on?"

He went and cut himself some soft sprigs, and we had to move Madame's hay a little to make room for the man in the hut. Then we lay around and burned pitch pine on the hearth and talked.

He didn't move on in the afternoon either, just lay around as though playing for time. When it started getting dark he went to the door opening and looked out at the weather. He asked back over his shoulder, "Do you think it'll snow tonight?"

"You ask me, and I ask you," I said. "But it looks like snow, the smoke's not rising."

That it might snow made him restless, he said he'd better leave tonight. Then suddenly he blew up. I was lying at my ease and had absentmindedly touched his bag with my hand again.

"I don't see what business you have with me," the man shouted, snatching the bag from me. "Stay away from my bag, I tell you!"

I told him I didn't mean anything by it, and that I wasn't going to steal anything from him.

"Steal, huh! So what? Perhaps you think I'm afraid of you? Forget it, my good man. Here's what I've got in the bag," the man said, starting to show me various things: three pairs of new mittens, some thick fabric for clothes, a bundle of groats, a flitch of bacon, sixteen twists of tobacco and a few big lumps of rock candy. At the bottom of the bag there was, maybe, a peck of coffee beans.

It was probably all of it merchandise from the general store, except for a heap of broken flatbread, which might have been pinched somewhere else.

"So you do have flatbread?" I said.

"If you had any sense you wouldn't talk like that," the man replied. "When I cross the mountain and have to walk and walk, won't I need something to stick in my mouth? It gives me the creeps to listen to you."

He packed everything carefully and neatly back into the bag, each article in turn. He took pains to stack the twists of tobacco up against the bacon, so that the cloth wouldn't get grease stains.

"I'd be happy to sell you the cloth," he said. "I'll give you a good price. It's duffel. It gets in my way."

"How much do you want for it?" I asked.

"There's enough for a whole suit, maybe more," he said to himself, spreading it out.

"Look," I said to the man, "here you come bringing the world and life and fancy ideas and newspapers into the forest. But let's talk a little. Tell me something: Are you afraid that somebody will see your footprints tomorrow if there's new snow tonight?"

"That's my business. I've crossed the mountain before and know plenty of trails," the man mumbled. "You can have the stuff for a few kroner."

I shook my head, and the man put the cloth neatly back in his bag just as if he owned it. "I'll cut it up for trousers," he said, "then it won't be so big and I'll be able to sell it."

"You would do better to allow for trousers, coat and vest from one piece," I said, "and cut the rest up for trousers."

"You think so? Yeah, maybe that's better."

We figured out how much would be needed for a

grown man's suit, using the string I'd tied up the letters with to measure our own clothes so as to get it right. Then we nicked the edge of the cloth and tore it across. Besides a complete suit there was material for two good-sized pairs of trousers.

Then the man offered to sell me other things from his bag, and I bought some coffee and a few twists of tobacco. He put the money in a leather wallet, and I saw how completely empty it was and noticed the pitiful, elaborate manner in which he put the money away and patted the outside of his pocket afterward.

"You weren't able to sell me very much," I said, "but I don't need anything else."

"A deal is a deal," he said, "I'm not complaining."

He was quite perky.

While he was getting ready to leave, no longer occupying his bed of pine sprigs, I couldn't help feeling sorry for him on account of his miserable little theft. A theft out of need: a flitch of bacon and a bit of cloth to try and sell in some forest. Oh, how theft has come down in the world! That is so partly because the punishment for all sorts of offenses has come down in the world. It's only a tiresome, humane punishment, the religious element has been removed from the law, a judge no longer has any mystique. I remember the last judge who explained

19

the meaning of the oath as it should be explained, to be effective. It made the hair stand on end on the lot of us. Give us a little magic again, and a little Sixth Book of Moses and the sin against the Holy Ghost and bonds signed in the blood of a newly christened child. And steal a bagful of cash and silverware from the store and hide it in the mountains, so that a blue flame will hover over the spot on autumn nights. But don't come to me with three pairs of mittens and a flitch of household bacon!

The man was no longer worried about his bag, he crawled all the way out of the hut to see where the wind was coming from. I put the tobacco and coffee I'd bought back in his bag again — I didn't need them. When he came in he said, "I think I'll take a chance and stay the night after all, if you don't mind."

In the evening he made no move to put out any of his own food. I made coffee and gave him some bread with it. "Don't go to any trouble," he said. Then he started fussing with his bag again, stowing the bacon well aside so it wouldn't damage the cloth, undid his belt, tied it diagonally around the bag and made a shoulder strap of it.

"Now, with the neck of the bag over the other shoulder, it'll be easier to carry," he said.

I gave him my letters to take along over the mountain and mail, and he tucked them safely away and slapped his pocket afterward. I put the postage money in a separate piece of paper for him, and he tied it up and fastened it to the neck of the bag.

"Where do you live?" I asked.

"Where can a poor devil live? I live on the coast. And I'm sorry to say I've got both a wife and kids, I can't deny it."

"How many kids do you have?"

"Four. And one of them has a broken arm and another — well, there's something wrong with all of them. So it's not so easy for a poor devil. The wife is sick, a few days ago she thought she was dying and had to receive the Sacrament."

A sad tone came into his voice. But the tone was false, he was lying through his teeth, of course. If someone came from the village to look for him, I dare say no Christian would have the heart to turn him in, since he had such a big family, and so sick. That must be what he was thinking.

Man, oh man, you're worse than a mouse!

I didn't inquire any further, but asked him to sing something, a ballad or a song, as long as we were sitting there anyway.

"I'm not in the mood for that now," he replied. "A hymn would be something else."

"Well, a hymn then."

"Not now. I would like to do you a favor, but."

He was getting more and more uneasy. In a little while he took his bag and went out. There he goes, I thought, without the customary goodbye: Rest easy! I did well going into the woods, I said to myself; here is my place, and from this day forth not another soul shall ever come within my walls.

I made a strict vow not to have anything more to do with people. "Come here, Madame," I said, "I honor you, Madame, and pledge to join my life to yours till death us do part."

Half an hour later the man came back. He didn't have the bag with him.

"I thought you'd gone," I said.

"Gone? I'm no dog," he replied. "I've been with people before, and I say 'Hello' when I arrive and 'Rest easy' when I go. Don't try to needle me."

"What did you do with your bag?"

"I've carried it part of the way."

He deserved credit for thinking ahead: he had rid himself of the bag in case something happened. It was easier to get away scot-free without a load on one's back. To keep him from telling me any more lies about his misery, I said, "I bet you were a real powerhouse a few years ago, eh? Probably still are, for that matter."

"Oh sure, considering my circumstances," he said, animated. "I never saw anyone lift a barrel of cod-liver oil more easily than I did, and nobody could match me on the dance floor at Christmas time. Ssh — is someone coming?"

We listened. In a second he had sized up the door opening and the hole in the roof and decided to meet the danger at the door. He was taut and splendid, I saw his jawbone working.

"It's nothing," I said.

Bold and strong like the devil, he crawled out of the hut and was away for several minutes. When he came back in, he drew a sigh of relief and said, "It was nothing."

We lay down for the night. "Well, then, in Jesus' name," he said, settling on his bed of pine sprigs. I fell asleep right off and slept soundly for a while. But later in the night the man's anxiety again brought him to his feet; I heard him mumble, "Rest easy" and crawl out.

In the morning I burned the man's pile of ever-greens and filled the hut with delicious pine smoke.

And outside there was new snow.

III

There is nothing like being alone again and walking around in the forest, turned in upon yourself and at peace. Making coffee and stuffing your pipe and leisurely mulling over things the while. Now I'm filling the kettle with snow, I think, and now I'm grinding these coffee beans with a stone; later I have to beat my sleeping bag thoroughly in the snow until the wool turns white again. There is nothing of literature or great novels or public opinion in any of this, and so what? But I didn't run a race in order to warm my gullet with this coffee. Literature? When Rome ruled the world it was, after all, merely Greece's babbling apprentice in literature. But Rome ruled the world. Or consider another country we know of: it fought a war of independence that is still bathed in glory, it produced the greatest painting in the world. But it had no literature and has none yet. . . .

Day by day I learn more and more about the trees and the moss and the snow on the ground, and all things become my friends. A pine stump is thawing in the sun, I feel a growing intimacy with it, at times I'm fond of it, something stirs in my soul. The bark is badly shredded, the stump was mutilated some winter in deep snow, that's why it sticks up so tall and naked. I put myself in this pine stump's place and look compassionately at it. And my eyes have, perhaps, the same simple animal expression that human eyes had in fossil times.

Now you'll see your chance to parody me, you can say lots of amusing things about this pine stump and me. And yet, deep down you know that in this, as in everything else, I have an edge on you, except that I don't have as much academic knowledge, nor am I a student, heh-heh. About field and forest you can teach me nothing, there I feel what no man has felt.

It happens sometimes that I make a wrong turn and lose my way. Oh yes, that happens. But I don't begin to spin and get lost right in front of my door, like you townfolks. I have to be twelve miles out of the way, far off on the other side of the Skjel River, before that happens, and then only on a sunless day, with heavy driving snow and no north or south to the sky. Then it's important to know about the marks and signs on this kind of tree and that, about the resin of the pine, the bark of the leafy trees, the moss growing down at the root, the angle of the branches facing north and south, how the rocks get overgrown with moss, how the network of veins in the leaves looks. With all this I can find my way as long as there is still some daylight.

But if dusk comes on, then I realize it's impossible to find my way home that day, and Christ, how will I pass the night! I say to myself. I stumble around till I find a snug place — best is a crag with shelter from wind and weather. I bring a few armfuls of pine sprigs, button up my jacket and make do for quite a while. Those who haven't tried it cannot know the subtle pleasure that thrills one's heart on such a night, when one sits in one's own snug hiding place. For something to do I light my pipe, but since I'm too hungry I can't stand the tobacco, so I stick a bit of resin into my mouth and chew on that, while thinking of one thing and another. And outside the snow continues to fly; if I've been lucky and my shelter faces the right way, the snow may drift closer and closer till it ends up forming a roof over my dwelling. Then I feel perfectly safe and fear neither to sleep nor wake; there will be no frostbite on my feet.

*

Two men came to my hut, they were in a hurry and one of them called out to me, "Good morning. Did a man go by here yesterday?"

I didn't like his face, I wasn't his servant and his question was too stupid.

"Lots of people may have gone by here. You must

mean did I *see* a man go by yesterday?"

There I gave it to him!

"I said what I meant," the man said angrily. "And besides, I'm asking in the name of the law."

"Really?"

I didn't want to talk anymore and crawled into the hut.

The two men followed. The Sheriff grinned and asked, "So, did you *see* a man go by here yesterday?"

"No," I replied.

They looked at each other and talked it over between them, and after a little while they left the hut and headed back to the village.

I thought, What professional vigilance this sheriff showed, how he sparkled with mediocrity! There would be bonuses for the arrest and transport of the prisoner, he would also reap honor for having accomplished his mission. Oh, all mankind ought to adopt this fellow, for he is its own son, created in its image! Where were the handcuffs? He ought to have rattled the chains a bit, lifted them onto his arm like the train of a riding habit, and made me feel something at the appalling power he had to clap somebody in irons. Nothing.

And what shopkeepers, what captains of commerce, we have nowadays! They instantly miss what a man can carry off in a bag and report it to the Sheriff.

From now on I'm looking forward to the spring. My turf hut still sits too close to people, and when the ground thaws I'll build myself another. I've picked out a place in the woods, on the far side of the Skjel River, where I think I'll be comfortable.

It's twenty-five miles to the village from there and almost twenty over the mountain.

IV

Did I say I was too close to people? Worse luck; for several days running I've taken a turn into the forest, saying good morning and pretending I was in human company. If it was a man I thought I had before me, we carried on a long, intelligent conversation, but if it was a woman I was polite: May I carry your bag, miss? Once it must have been the Lapp's daughter I thought I met, for I was lavish with flattery and offered to carry her fur coat if she would take it off and go naked, tee-hee.

I guess I'm no longer too close to people, worse luck. And I guess I won't build that turf hut still more out of the way.

The days are getting longer and I won't complain

about that. The fact is I've suffered great hardship this winter and learned to discipline myself. It occupied my time, and it required a certain strength of will occasionally. I have to say I've paid dearly for my education. Sometimes I was unnecessarily hard on myself. There is a loaf of bread, I said, it doesn't surprise me, it doesn't interest me, I'm used to it. But now you'll see no bread for twelve hours, then it will make an impression on you, I said, and hid the loaf.

That was this winter.

Were they difficult days? No, good days. I was so free, I could do and think what I liked, I was alone, a bear in the woods. But even in the middle of the forest people dare not talk aloud without looking about them, they rather walk in silence. For a while you console yourself that it is very English to be silent, that it is regal to be silent; but one day it goes too far, your tongue wakes up and stretches and suddenly you holler an idiocy or two: "Bricks for the palace! The calf is much healthier today!" If done well it can be heard for a mile and a half — and then you stand there and feel a stinging pain as if slapped. If only you had kept your regal silence! It happened that the postman who crosses the mountain once a month surprised me the moment I had shouted. "What?" he asked from the trees. "Watch out, I've rigged a cocked gun down there," I answered, to save face.

But with the long days my courage has grown, it must be the spring that triggers it, this mysterious upsurge within me; now I no longer worry about a shout more or less. I clatter extra loud with my pots and pans when I cook, while singing at the top of my voice. It's the spring.

Yesterday I stood on a hill and looked out over the winter woods. The trees have taken on another aspect now, they've grown gray and dreary, and the midday sun has melted much of the snow and pressed it together. Catkins are everywhere, they lie in heaps under the young trees, like scrambled letters of the alphabet. The moon rises, stars pop out, I'm cold and shiver a little, but since there's nothing to do in the hut, I prefer to stand here shivering as long as possible. This winter I did nothing so foolish, then I went home when I was cold, now I'm bored with that too. It's the spring.

Ah, the sky is clear and cool, lying wide open to all the stars. There is a multitude of worlds up on that immense plain, they are so small and teeming, so tinklingly small; gazing at them I seem to hear a thousand tiny bells. Yes, everything draws my thoughts in a definite direction: toward spring and the pastures.

V

I pile wood on the fire, take all my gear on my back and leave the hut. "Goodbye, Madame."

Yes, that's how it ended.

I feel no joy at parting with my lodging, if anything a little sadness — as always when leaving a place that has been my home for a long time. But the whole world was calling me from out there. Yes, I'm just like all other lovers of forests and open spaces: we tacitly agreed to meet again, last night it was — suddenly I felt my eyes gliding toward the door as I sat there.

I turn a few times to look back at the hut; smoke rises from the roof, it puffs and waves to me and I wave back.

I feel refreshed by the clear, silky tone in the air, the sun slowly begins to rise in a long, long blue patch of sky beyond the forest. The dawn looks like a cheerful pirate coast in the sky before me. The mountains are all on my left.

After a few hours walking I am like new from top to toe, all is going well. I brandish my stick in the air and it swishes "ho"; when I think I've earned it I sit down and eat.

You certainly have none of my joys in town.

I strut along, full of life and spirit, on the point of

whooping and hollering. I pretend my load weighs nothing at all, leap about needlessly and overexert myself a bit; but it's easy to put up with overexertion when you're driven to it by inner contentment. Here in my solitude, many miles from people and houses, I experience childlike states of carefree happiness that you cannot possibly understand, unless you get someone to explain them to you. Listen: striking a pose, I pretend I've just noticed a remarkable kind of tree. At first I don't pay much attention to it, but after a little while I stick out my neck and squint and stare. What? I say to myself, could it really be —! I say. I throw down my load and go closer, I examine the tree and nod; sure, it's one of a kind, a fabulous tree, I have discovered it! And I take out my notebook and describe the tree.

Just a joke, just fun, an odd little impulse — I play. Children have done it before me. And here there's no postman to take me by surprise. But I quit the game as suddenly as I began it, as children do. For a moment, though, I was carried back to the dear, foolish bliss of childhood.

I wonder if it was the joy of soon seeing people again that made me so playful.

The next day I come to the Lapp's place, just as a raw fog settles on mountain and forest. I go in. And there nothing but good things happen to me, but there's no fun in a Lapp hut. Horn spoons and knives line the turf wall, and a small kerosene lamp hangs from the ceiling. The Lapp himself is a dull nonentity, he can neither discover lost things nor cast a spell anymore. His daughter is on the other side of the mountain, she has gone to the school for settled Lapps and can read but not write. The two elders, husband and wife, are pure imbeciles. Common to the whole family is an animal dumbness; if I ask something I may or may not get a tiny little answer back: M-no, m-yes. I was not a Lapp, they mistrusted me.

The fog lay over the forest all afternoon, covering it with hoarfrost. I gave myself a nap. In the evening the sky cleared again, there were a few degrees of frost. I stepped out of the hut, the full moon loomed huge and silent over the earth.

Oh, bother — those untuned strings!

But where are all the little birds,
and where have I strayed myself?
I stand in a world of silver coves
where nothing comes and nothing goes
and nothing ever betides.
I stare and see no place I know
wherever I turn my eyes.

And so he came to a silver wood —
thus went a fairy tale.
There hung a tune in the shimmering air
as if sung by a starry choir.
If only I'd come as a blooming lad
and turned the wily troll to stone
for to waken a slumbering maid.

Today I smile at fairy tales,
old age has made me wise.
Time was I moved with prodigal rage,
now my feet are heavy with age,
while my heart — my heart wants to leap.
I'm driven by fire and bound by ice
and can find no rest or sleep.

A shudder flashes from the evening sky
as before a soul is released.
A breath stirs the forest's silver lace,
as though a lion with mighty pace
streaked by on padded paws.
Maybe some god on his evening walk.
And the forest trembled in its repose.

When I got back to the hut the daughter had come
home, she was getting something to eat after her long

walk. Olga Lapp, small and quaint, sexed-up in a snowbank saying how-de-do. *Boris!* they said and took a tumble. Now she had bought herself some red and blue patches of fabric at the village store, and no sooner had she eaten than she pushed the dishes away and began to decorate her Sunday jacket with the pretty fabrics. Through it all she never utters a word, because a Norwegian is present.

"You know me, don't you, Olga?"

"M-yes."

"But you look so angry."

"M-no."

"How was the trail over the mountain?"

"Good."

I knew of the abandoned turf hut the family had lived in before and asked, "How far is it to your old hut?"

"It's not far," Olga answered.

Ah, Olga Lapp is sure to have someone to smile at, if not exactly me. Here she sits in the vast forest giving in to her vanity, sewing some gorgeous trimmings on her jacket. On Sunday she will probably go to church and meet the one who is meant to admire it.

I didn't care to stay with these small creatures, these runts, any longer, and since I'd had a good sleep in the afternoon and the moon was shining brightly outside, I was ready to go. As soon as I had stocked up on reindeer cheese and any other foodstuff I could get, I stepped out. But a surprise awaited me: there was no bright moonlight anymore, but an overcast sky; there was no frost either, but mild weather and wet woods. It was the spring.

Olga Lapp advised me not to go when she saw how it was; but why should I listen to her twaddle? She came with me a little way into the forest, to the right path, then turned and went back, small and quaint, like a bedraggled hen.

VI

It was a struggle moving on — oh, well! Hours later I find myself high up in the mountains, I must have lost my way. What's that darkness over there? A mountain peak. That darkness over there? Another peak. Let's pitch camp right here.

Nonetheless there was a deep goodness and a softness to the mild night. I sat in the dark and brought forth forgotten memories of childhood and many adventures from here and there. What a satisfaction it is, though, to have money in your pocket even if you lie under the open sky!

I wake up during the night from being too warm under my crag, I have to unbuckle my sleeping bag; besides, a sound seems to linger in my ear, maybe I shouted or sang in my sleep. All at once I'm well rested and start looking around. It's dark and mild, a silent world of stone. I look at the slightly lighter sky and, nearby, a ring of mountains all around; I'm in a city of mountain peaks, lying at the foot of a cliff so enormous as to seem deformed. The wind begins to blow, and suddenly a rumble is heard far off. What weather! Then there is a flash of lightning, followed by thunder, which slides like a huge avalanche down among the farthest mountains. It's marvelous to lie there listening, delightful to the point of perversity, a wave of delight floods through me; I get sort of drunk in a strange, wild way I've never experienced before, expressing itself by my laughing, being wanton and humorous. I'm struck by one fancy after another and pleasantries occur to me, with moments in between of such great sorrow that I lie there gasping for air. There is another flash of lightning, the thunder is closer; it begins to rain, it pours, the echoes are very loud, all nature is in an uproar, pandemonium. I try to overpower the night by shouting into it, lest it mysteriously drain all my strength and sap my will. You'll see, these mountains are all sheer spells against my journey, I think to myself, huge planted curses to block my way. Or have I just stumbled into the mountains' trade union? But I nod several times, which should mean I'm feeling bold and cheerful. Maybe the mountains are only stuffed.

More lightning and thunder and downpour, the near echo is like a blow — that did it! flashes through me. Oh well, I've read about many a battle and been under fire before this! Then, in a moment of sadness and humility amid all this might, I whimper and think, What, or who, am I at this moment? Or maybe I'm lost, so that I'm nothing anymore! And I jabber and call out my name to hear if it exists.

Then — a golden wheel spins in front of me and the thunder cracks directly overhead, over my own mountain. I'm out of my sleeping bag and my shelter in a trice, the rumble rolls on, there is more thunder and lightning, it's tearing worlds up by the roots. Why didn't I listen to little Olga and stay where I was, in the hut! It's probably the Lapp casting his spell! The Lapp? Huh, that runt, that mountain shrimp — but this is me! What does all this crashing have to do with me? I make a halfhearted attempt to go on in spite of it but give up; I find myself among giants, and I see how foolish it would be to try a scuffle with thunder.

I lean against the rock wall and do not challenge or yell at my opponent; on the contrary, I look on him with milk-blue eyes. And now that I have surrendered, nothing except a mountain could be so hard. As you please. But I'm certainly not all verse and tuneful rhythms, how can you think I would ruin my brains with such rainbows? That's a lie. I stand here leaning against the *world*, that's all, though you probably take the blue in my eyes for the real thing. . . .

Then I myself was struck by lightning. It was a wonder, and it happened to me. It went along my left elbow and singed my coat sleeve; the lightning seemed like a ball of yarn, it rolled. Feeling a heat, I saw the ground further down getting ripped open with a loud clap, a force knocked me down and a shaft of darkness went through me. Then the thunder grew excessively loud, not long and rumbling but firm and clear, crackling.

The storm drove over.

VII

The next day I came to the abandoned hut, wet to the skin, lightning-struck, but feeling strangely mild and easygoing, as though I had been chastised. My luck in the disaster made me feel extra kindly toward everything, I tramped along without hurting the mountain and refrained from thinking sinful thoughts, even though it was springtime. It didn't even annoy me that I had to retrace my steps down the mountain to find the path to the hut again; I could afford the time, there was no need to hurry. I was the first spring tourist and all too early.

I lie around the hut for a few days and feel good. Sometimes at night lines of verse and little poems came into my head, as though I had become a regular poet. In any case, it showed how much I had changed inside since the winter, when all I cared for was to lie about blinking my eyes and being left alone.

One fine sunny day during the thaw I left the hut and took to the mountain, where I roamed about for several hours. I had lately thought of writing some nursery rhymes addressed to a special little girl, but it hadn't come to anything. Now, on the mountain, I felt like going back to this pastime and took several turns working at it, but the result wasn't good enough. Well, it's probably at night, after a couple of hours sleep, that such things come.

Then I went straight to the village and bought myself a goodly load of provisions. There were many people in those parts, and it did me good to hear human speech and laughter again; but it wasn't a place where I could stay, and anyway I'd come too early. On my way back to the hut I was carrying a heavy load. About halfway I met a man, an idle laborer, a vagabond named Solem. Later I learned he was the illegitimate son of a telegraph operator who lived at Rosenlund almost a generation ago.

The very fact that this man stepped aside to let me by with my load was a nice trait, and I thanked him and said, "No need, I won't run over you anyway, heh-heh."

After I got past him, the man asked about the condition of the road to the village. I told him it was the same as here. "Oh, uh-huh," he said, and was about to go. It occurred to me that he might have come some distance, and since he wasn't carrying anything that looked like food, I offered him some of mine so I could talk to him a bit. He thanked me and took what I offered.

He was above average height, quite young, in his late twenties or maybe thirty, a sturdy fellow. A tuft of hair stuck out from under the visor of his cap, in the jaunty manner of a vagabond; but he had no beard. This full-grown man still shaved himself, he hadn't grown tired of it; that and the forelock and his whole manner gave me the impression that he wanted to pass for younger than he was.

We chatted while he ate. He laughed easily and was of good cheer, and since his face was beardless and hard it was like iron laughing. But he was sensible and engaging. Only, I'd been silent for so long that I may have talked a bit too readily; if we both happened to say something at the same time, this Solem fellow and I, he stopped at once and let me have the first word. After this was repeated a few times I was no longer interested in winning and stopped as well. But he just nodded and said, "Please, go on."

I told him I was on a hike, during which I fooled around and studied interesting trees and wrote a trifle about them now and then, that I was staying in a turf hut but had just run out of food, so that a trip to the village had been necessary. When he heard about the hut he stopped chewing and seemed just to listen, then said quickly, "You know, these telegraph poles over the mountain, in a way I'm quite familiar with them. Well, not exactly these here, but other poles. I was a lineman till just recently."

"Were you?" I said, following up by asking, "You passed my hut today, didn't you?"

He hesitated a moment, but when he saw that I wasn't out to get him, he admitted having dropped by the hut and rested, and there he had found my flatbread. "It wasn't easy to sit there without taking a little of it," he said.

We talked about various things; his way of expressing himself was so wonderfully free of crudities, and he didn't make a mess when he ate. I was only semi-educated myself and appreciated his good manners.

He offered to help me carry part of the way as a thank-you for the food, and I accepted his offer. And so, as it turned out, this stranger went along with me all the way back to the hut. As soon as I entered I noticed a slip of paper on the table, a sort of thanks for the flatbread, a dreadfully vulgar, coarsely worded note. When Solem saw what I was reading, his iron face broke into a smile. I pretended I didn't understand a word of it and threw the note back on the table; he took it and tore it up.

"I'm very sorry you saw that," he said. "We linemen get into the way of doing things like that, I simply forgot I'd left it there."

Soon after he went outside.

He stayed the night and the next day; he found an excuse to wash some clothes for me, making himself useful as far as he could, poor fellow. A large caldron had been sitting outside the hut since the time of the Lapps; it was cracked and leaked badly, but Solem sealed it with bacon fat and boiled my clothes in it. It was a very comical sight; whenever the fat floated up he just skimmed it off.

He seemingly intended to stay till we ran out of food again and then go with me to the village, but when he heard I had decided to go in the opposite direction, to a mountain farm, a place at the foot of the Tore Peaks which took in summer guests and where many travelers came by, he wanted to come with me. He was nothing if not free as a bird.

"Then you'll let me come along and carry things, won't you?" he said. "I'm an experienced farm hand, too, maybe they'll give me something to do."

VIII

The big farm was already alive with spring, men and beasts had awoken, the cow barn was filled with a nonstop moo all day long; the goats had long since been put out to pasture.

It was a good way to the nearest neighbor; a cotter or two had cleared holdings in the forest which they had since bought, otherwise all one saw belonged to the farm. Many new buildings had gone up as the traffic over the mountain increased, gargoyles gaped, Norwegian and homey, from the gables, and a piano was playing in the common room with the fireplace. Do you recognize it? You've been here, after all, the farm folks have been asking about you.

Fine days, fine days once more, a fitting transition from solitude. I talk to the young couple who now own the place, and with the husband's old father and his young sister, Josephine. The old man comes out of his room and looks me over. He's frightfully old, maybe ninety, his eyes are tired, with a sort of insane look. He himself has shrunk to nothing, and each time he drags himself into the light of day, with the help of both hands, it's as though he emerges from the womb again to find a new world before him: Have you ever seen the likes, there are some buildings on the farm! he thinks, looking at them. And when the barn doors are open he looks that way too, thinking, Have you ever seen the likes, it reminds me of a door opening, what can it be? It really looks like a door opening. . . . And he stands and stares at it a long time.

But Josephine, a daughter from his last marriage, is young and plays the piano for me. Ah, Josephine! When she hurries across the yard her feet are a blur under her skirt. She is so kind to strangers, I'm pretty sure she discovered Solem and me from afar as we came walking, and pounced on the piano. She has such poor, pale young-girl hands, they confirm my old observation that the look of the hands has something to do with sex, that it reveals chastity, indifference, or libido. It's fun to watch Josephine milk a goat, straddling the animal. But that sort of chore she does only for show these days, to please the guests; usually she can't take time from her indoor work for such things, heavens no — she waits at table and waters the flowers and converses with me about who climbed the Tore Peaks last year and who the year before, does Miss Josephine.

So I bustle about, refreshed and renewed, stand awhile watching Solem, who has been set to carting manure, and then wander off through the woods to the cotters' plots. Nice houses, a barn for two cows and a few goats at each place, half-naked children with homemade toys outside, quarrels and laughter and tears. The men at both plots cart out the manure on sledges, they find a trail where snow and ice still cover the ground and it goes very well. I don't go down to the houses but survey the work from the hill where I stand. I know the life of labor well, oh yes, and like it.

It was no small area these cotters had cleared, regular little farms just the right size; and, what's more, the fence around the home fields reached a good way into the woods. They would be home to five cows and a horse, these places, when the area was cleared all the way to the fence.

Good luck!

The days go by. The windowpanes have thawed, the snow is melting, it's getting green by the sunny walls, the woods are leafing out. I still hold to my original intention of making great irons red-hot within me; but I would be incredibly ridiculous if I thought this an easy task. I don't even know for certain whether the irons are still there, nor do I know whether I can forge them myself anymore, even if I have them. Since this winter life has made me lonely and small, I putter around here remembering how once it was different. Now that I've come out into the light of day and to people again, I've begun to realize all this. I was a different horseman once: the wave has its crest, so had I; the wine has its glow, so had I. And neurasthenia, the mimic of all diseases, shadows me.

So what? Oh, nothing, and so I don't grieve over it. Grieve? Grieving is for women. Life is a loan, I give thanks for the loan. I have now and then had gold and silver and copper and iron and other lesser metals, and the world was great fun, much more fun than some out-of-the-way life in eternity; but the fun cannot continue. I don't know anyone who hasn't fared just as badly as I have, but I don't know anyone who will admit it. Oh, how it went downhill with them! But even so they said, Just look how we're still going uphill! At their first jubilee they left life behind and began to vegetate; the seventies begin at fifty. And the irons were red no more, and there were no irons. But, God help me, every simple soul declared the irons were there, and that the irons were red. Just look at these irons! the simple souls said, look how red they are! they said.

As though the important thing was to keep death away for another twenty years from someone who had already begun to die! I don't understand such thinking, but maybe you do with your cheerful banality and your book learning. A one-armed man can still walk, a one-legged man can still lie down. And what did you learn about the forest? What did *I* learn *in* the forest? *That young trees grow there.*

Behind me stands youth, which the boneheads and the rabble disparage to the point of shamelessness and barbarism simply because it's young. I've seen it for many years. I know nothing more contemptible than your book learning and the way you judge things by it. Whether you chart your life with a catechism or a pair of compasses, it's all the same; come here, my little friend, and I'll present you with a pair of compasses from my latest iron.

IX

A tourist came to us, the first tourist. The farmer himself escorted him over the mountain, and Solem went along so he could guide others later. Short and stout and thin-haired, the stranger stood in the yard, a well-to-do elderly man who hiked for his health and for the sake of those last twenty years. Poor Josephine turned her feet into a blur under her skirt and showed him into the room with the fireplace, the piano and the china. When he left, his small change turned up, and Josephine accepted it with her pale girlish hand. On the other side of the mountain Solem got a two-krone piece for the trip, and that was good money. Everything went so well, the farmer himself was also pleased: "Now they'll start coming," he said. "If they would only leave us alone," he added.

With this last remark he was thinking of the good, carefree days he and his house had enjoyed until now; but in a few weeks a motorcar service was scheduled to open in the neighboring valley, and then the tourist traffic might be diverted there. His wife and Josephine were a bit worried already, but the farmer himself had thought otherwise as long as possible: at any rate they had the regular guests who came back year after year and would never change! Anyway, let them get all the motorcars they wanted, those other places, they didn't have the Tore Peaks!

The farmer had been so sure he was right that, once again, he had plenty of timber stacked up by the wall of the barn, ready for putting up new buildings — six additional guest rooms, a hall with reindeer antlers and log chairs, and a bath. But what had got into him today, was he having second thoughts? If they would only leave us alone! he said.

A week later Mrs. Brede arrived with her children, she was given her own cottage as in previous years. She must be rich and genteel, this Mrs. Brede, to get her own cottage. She was a gracious lady, and the little girls were tall, attractive children. They curtsied to me, and I don't know why, but it was like getting flowers. An odd feeling.

But then came Miss Torsen and Mrs. Molie, who were both regular guests, and then Mr. Staur, a teacher, who was to stay a week. Later came Miss Johnsen and Miss Palm, both schoolteachers, and still later Master Høy, a high school teacher, and some others — businessmen, telephone operators, folks from Bergen, a Dane or two. We were many at table and had lively conversations. When Staur was offered more soup he replied in his New Norwegian brogue, "No thanks, I do not care for any more!" signifying to us all as he cast his eyes around that this was the way it should be said. Outside of mealtimes we got together and wandered in the woods or in the mountains, some here, others there. But few transient guests turned up, or none at all, and those were the ones needed to make a profit, from rooms rented by the night and from individual meals and coffee. Josephine had lately seemed worried, and her young fingers grew more and more greedy when they counted silver coins.

Lean brook trout, goat ragout and canned goods. Some of the guests were dissatisfied and talked about leaving, others praised both the food and the mountain scenery. Miss Torsen, the schoolteacher, wanted to leave. She was quite tall and attractive, with a red hat setting off her dark hair; but there were no suitable young men here, and in the long run it grew tiresome to completely waste one's vacation. Mr. Batt, a businessman who'd been both to Africa and America, was the sole candidate, for even the Bergen folk were good for nothing. "Where's Miss Torsen?" Batt would ask. "Here, I'm coming," she answered. They didn't like to hike in the mountains but preferred the woods, where they could lie and chat for long spells. Oh, but apparently Batt wasn't much good either; he was short and freckled and talked only about money and profit. Anyway, the shop he had in town seemed to be quite small, one selling cigars and fruit. No, he couldn't be much good.

One day, during a rainy spell, I had a long conversation with Miss Torsen. A strange young woman, generally proud and quiet but sometimes expansive and eager, a bit reckless too. We were sitting in the common room and people came and went the whole time, but she didn't lower her voice on that account; quite the contrary, she spoke in a high, clear voice, occasionally folding her hands and pulling them apart again in her eagerness. After we'd been there awhile, Batt came in too, listened to her for a moment and said, "I'm going now, Miss Torsen, are you coming?" She merely gave him the once-over, turned away and went on talking. She looked very proud and determined. All in all she seemed to be a capable young woman; she was twenty-seven, she said, and fed up with her schoolmistress' life.

Why had she started that life anyway?

"Oh, fashion," she replied. "The girls nearby were also choosing the path of learning, as they called it, studying languages and learning grammar, it was so great. We were going to be independent and make lots of money. Don't you believe it! I would gladly have given it up for a home of my own, however small. And the drudgery during all those years at school!

Some of the girls were well-to-do, but those of us who were poor didn't have the clothes they did, and we didn't have nice hands like they did. And so we wound up ducking all work at home for the sake of our hands. We also put on airs for the boys in class. They were gentlemen in our eyes — one had a saddle horse, a regular fool by the way, but another was a millionaire's son and terribly nice; he gave away money to us, to me I mean, and he often kissed me. His name was Flaten, his father was a businessman. Since he was so handsome and elegant, we wanted to look chic to him in return. He could have asked me anything he liked, I prayed to God for him. Many probably thought the same as me: Were we chic? Were we good-looking? That's how our days were spent. We left the washing and cooking and mending to our mothers and sisters, we students had to just sit and grow learned and have angelic hands. We were crazy, of course, I really mean it. In those years we picked up misconceptions we would be burdened with for the rest of our lives; we became stupid with book learning, anemic, unbalanced: sometimes terribly sad about our lot and sometimes hysterically happy and stuck-up about our degrees, our refinement. We were the pride of our families. And we were independent, oh sure! We got office jobs, forty kroner a month.

Because there was nothing remarkable about being a student anymore, we weren't a rarity now, there were hundreds of us, so we got only forty kroner a month. Of that, thirty went to our parents for upkeep and ten to ourselves. It was nothing. We needed to wear nice clothes at work and, young as we were, we loved to stroll about town; but we couldn't afford any of it and went into debt, while some of us got engaged to guys no better off than ourselves. That pent-up life in school during our youth had other unwholesome effects on us too. We wanted to show some spirit, of course, and not flinch from any experience, and so things went badly for a number of us; some got married and not surprisingly, in view of the circumstances, turned into conspicuous failures in their homes, while others disappeared to America. But they probably all continue to be proud of their languages and their degrees. It's all they have got — neither joy nor health nor innocence, but a college degree. Good God!"

"But some of you did become teachers, with good salaries?"

"Good salaries? The fact is, we had to start our studying all over again. As if our fathers and mothers and brothers and sisters hadn't sacrificed enough for our sakes already! More cramming again over a long period, before we were ready to start our lives in the classroom — bequeathing to others the same unnatural youth we'd had ourselves. Oh sure, we had chosen a beautiful vocation, everyone thought so, it was almost like being a missionary. But now I won't go on with this beautiful vocation any longer, if I can find a way to get out. Anything else would be better."

Batt opens the door and says, "Are you coming, Miss Torsen? It has stopped raining."

"No, leave me alone!" she replied.

Batt withdrew.

"Why are you turning him away like that?" I asked.

"Because . . . It's really nasty outside," she replied, looking out. "Besides he's so stupid. And he's impertinent."

How sure of herself she looked, and how right she seemed to be!

Poor Miss Torsen! Whatever the facts of the matter were, word got around in the pension that Miss Torsen had recently lost her job, after they had put up with her eccentric teaching for a long time.

So that was it.

But what she had told me was probably just as true for all that.

X

Just imagine, the farmer is badly in debt, it turns out, and has let his cotters purchase fresh patches of arable land from him to raise cash. I'm becoming privy to a great many things now. Mrs. Brede strolls about with her lovely, gentle face and knows something about everything, all her summer sojourns at the place have made her wise. So when she speaks her mind about the situation she doesn't have to search for words.

Oh yes, the man is deeply in debt.

No one would guess that anything was wrong here; all the new buildings and flagpoles, the curtains on the windows and the red-painted well house — everything gives the impression of great prosperity. Nor are the interiors disappointing: I won't mention the piano, but there are paintings on the walls and photographs of the place from all sides, an ample subscription to newspapers and, strewn on the tables, a selection of novels, which aren't greatly missed when guests occasionally make off with them. Another thing: the bill comes on a handsomely printed form with a picture of the place against the background of the Tore Peaks. All in all one cannot doubt that there is money here. And one thinks: that wouldn't be surprising after running a health resort for tourists and boarders for twenty years.

But all the same the truth is that all this construction and all the furnishings inside and out cost more than the operation can bear. Mr. Brede, too, has money invested in the place, which is why Mrs. Brede is here every year with her children, eating up the dividends.

No wonder she has a house to herself, it's her own house, after all.

"Well, it was a good place in the old days," Mrs. Brede says, "travelers came here for meals and a roof over their heads, it cost nothing to run it then. But the traffic forced them to make improvements and to expand, they had to go along with progress, keep up with other such places in the country — they're all in a race, of course. And the owner here probably isn't the right person to run such an unstable, capricious business, he has developed too much of a taste for idling and leaving the farm to take care of itself. His two cotters now, they are enterprising fellows. They are the owner's cousins; they buy one piece of the farm after another and till it. My husband often says it will probably end with the cotters or their children buying the whole farm from Paul."

"How could cotters bring off something like that?"

"They work, they're peasants. They began in the woods here, one after the other, with three or four goats apiece; they went to work down in the village, bringing back food and money, and the whole time they were clearing their plots. Then came more goats and a cow, they bought more outlying fields, which meant still more cattle. They sow barley and plant potatoes and cultivate a garden; the people here buy root crops from their cotters, they have no time to toil and moil with such things, because that's a lot of work. No, on this farm they sow nothing but green forage for the cattle now, the rest doesn't pay, Paul says. And in a sense he's right. He did try hiring enough hands to run the farm, but it didn't work out. The tourists start coming right in the middle of the spring planting, and time and again every hired hand has to leave off work to escort tourists over the mountain or do one thing or another for the guests. And that's how it goes, all those short summer weeks; there have been years around here when they didn't even get all the manure out. Still, all things considered, it's worst in the fall, when the travelers are rushing to get back home, then it's impossible to get any harvesting done without being disturbed. My husband says it's almost a tradition here now that the cotters get to mow the outlying meadows for an even share of the yield."

When I showed surprise at Mrs. Brede knowing

so much about farming, she shook her head and admitted she didn't really understand much herself, she had it all from her husband. It just happened that every time the cotters bought another piece of land from Paul, her husband had to give his consent to the deal. On account of the mortgage. That was how they became involved. For that matter, Mr. Brede would just as soon get out of the affair, but it wasn't that easy; and now he was very anxious about the new motorcar service.

Mrs. Brede was a kind, gentle, maternal woman who played with her little girls and seemed to be wonderfully poised. Look at this, for example: one day one of the goats came home with a broken hind leg; all the guests rushed out with brandy and lanolin and bandages, but Mrs. Brede remained seated, full of experience, wise, and a bit surprised at all that zealousness. "There's usually nothing to do with a goat like that but slaughter it," she said.

She must have married early, I gathered, her two little girls were ten and twelve; her husband seemed to run a big business, spending much of the year in Iceland and generally traveling a lot. But she bore this too with composure. And yet she was still young and attractive, maybe a little plump for her height but with a fine skin, without a wrinkle. She was so unlike

Miss Torsen, our other beauty, who was tall and dark.

Ah, but I suspect Mrs. Brede wasn't always as calm as she looked. When she came down to the servants' quarters and asked Solem a favor one evening, I saw her blush and become unrecognizable. Could Solem come and put up a window shade that had fallen down? It was late in the evening, she seemed to have been in bed but had gotten up again, and Solem didn't appear very willing. Then their eyes suddenly met, they were glued together for a moment. Yeah, sure, he'd come. . . .

The iron roughneck, that damn Solem!

Mrs. Brede left.

Less than two minutes later she was back to call it off: Never mind, she would put up the shade herself.

XI

A few tourists came and went, Solem escorted them over the mountain and they were gone. But where were all the foreigners this year? Not a single one. Bennett's and Cook's caravans, the crowds bent on *doing* the mountain peaks of Norway, where were they?

Then two pitiful Englishmen showed up. They were middle-aged, unshaven, and sloppy altogether, two engineers or whatever they were, but as mute and rude as the most genteel of those traveling English jack-asses. "Guide? Guide?" they shouted. "You're the guide, yes?" Nothing about them was any different from what we'd seen before: the two of them were traveling, earnestly and foolishly, in search of mountain peaks; they were in a hurry, on a serious errand, as though they were looking for a doctor. Solem guided them to the top and down the other side, they offered him a twenty-five øre piece. He told me later he had kept his hand out, thinking they would count out more, but nothing came. Then he made a stink — oh yes, the fellow had already become thoroughly demoralized and shameless from idling among tourists! "*Mehr, more,*" he said. They turned a deaf ear. Solem threw the coin on the ground and smacked his hands together a few times. That helped, a one-krone piece appeared. But when Solem grabbed the lord by the shoulder and threw a bit of weight into it, he got two kroner. "You crumb!" Solem said.

Finally a caravan came. Mixed tongues, both sexes, hunters, anglers, dogs, mountain climbers, porters. A huge commotion arose; the flag was run up, Paul was bent double under all the requests, and Josephine ran, ran at every beckoning. Mrs. Brede had to turn her cottage over to three *ladies*, and the rest of us were squeezed together as best we could. As for me, I could keep my bed because of my age, but I answered, "No way, let this English lawyer or whatever he is have my bed, what difference does one night make to me!"

And out I went.

One can observe a good deal during the day at a health resort, if one keeps one's eyes open. And one can observe a good deal at night. That bleating in the goatshed, what's behind all that? Why haven't the animals settled in for the night? The door is shut, no strange dogs have slipped in. Have no strange dogs slipped in? Vice runs in circles, in cycles, just like virtue, I suddenly begin to reflect, nothing is new, everything comes around again and repeats itself. Rome ruled the world, to be sure. Oh, they were so mighty, those Romans, so invincible; they allowed themselves a vice or two, they could afford to live it up at the arena, they had their fun with boys and animals. Then one day retribution started coming down on them, their grandchildren lost a battle here and a battle there, and their grandchildren in turn only sat looking back. The circle closed, none ruled the world less than Rome.

They paid no attention to me, the two Englishmen in the goatshed; I was just one of the natives, a Norwegian, I had to hold my tongue before the mighty tourists. But they themselves belonged to that

nation of runners, coachmen, and vice which a salu-
tary fate in the guise of Germany will some day chas-
tise unto death. . . .

The commotion at the farm continued all night;
the hunting dogs started in very early, the caravan
awoke at six, doors began slamming all over the
premises. They were in a hurry, those travelers, they
were off to the doctor. They ate breakfast in two
shifts, but though their hosts bent double and gave
of their best, not everyone was satisfied. "If we'd
only known about you a little earlier," Paul said.
But they mumbled back, "Just wait, certain other
places are getting motorcars now!" Then Paul,
master of his own farm, the man at the foot of the
Tore Peaks, said, "But I'm going to build more;
don't you see all that timber outside? And I've also
been thinking of getting a telephone. . . ."

The caravan simply paid the little they owed and
left; the master and Solem both helped carry their
bags.

And so it grew quiet around us again.

Staur, the teacher, also left. He'd been held up by
collecting plants around the Tore Peaks; at table he
spoke about his plants and was very learned, gave the
Latin names and pointed out their peculiarities —
oh, he'd learned so much at the teachers college. "Here

you see *Artemis cotula*," he would say.

Miss Torsen, who had also acquired much learning, thought for a moment and remarked, "Right you are, take plenty of that one with you."

"Why?"

"It's insect powder."

Staur knew nothing about that, it caused a bit of a stir and Master Høy had to butt in.

No, Staur knew nothing about that. But he knew how to classify plants and to memorize their names. That was so much fun, he thought. Peasant children in his district didn't know those classes or names, and so he could teach them. It was such fun.

But was the *genius loci* his friend? The plant that is cut, cut right off one year to grow back again the next, did this marvel render him religious and still? What about the stones and the heather and the slender roots of trees, and the grass and the forest and the wind and the vast sky over the world — were they his friends? *Artemis cotula* . . .

XII

When I get tired of Master Høy and the women . . .
Now and then I think about Mrs. Molie. She's sewing, and Høy keeps her dignified company; they talk about their maids at home who only want to stay out at night. Mrs. Molie is a thin, flat-chested woman, but I don't suppose she has always been so unpleasant to look at. Her bluish teeth look cold, as though made of ice, but a few years ago maybe her husband knew nothing so beautiful as her full mouth with its dark down at the corners. Ah yes, her husband. Well, he's a sailor, a skipper, home only now and then to add to the family, otherwise he's off to Australia, to China, to Mexico. It's howdy and goodbye with him. And here is the wife, for the sake of her health. I wonder if she's here solely for her health, or if she and Høy, in their heart of hearts, aren't from the same small town.

When I get tired of Master Høy and the women, I abandon them and go out. And then I'm out all day and no one knows where I keep myself. It becomes a man of a certain age to be different from Høy, who has far to go to reach such mature years. Yes, I go out. It's clear weather and just warm enough, I scent the fragrance of the plants in my summer woods. I take frequent rests, not because I need to but because the earth is so loving. I go far enough so that no one can find me, and then I'm safe. No sound of the farm or people, no one in sight, only this overgrown little goat trail with a bit of green at the edges and so nice. A tiny stub of a goat trail, it looks as if it has fallen asleep here in the woods, so thin and alone; here it lies.

You who read this probably feel nothing, but I who sit here and write sense a kind of sweetness just by recalling a path in the woods. It was like meeting a child.

My hands under my head and my nose in the air, I let my eyes meander across the sky. High up over the Tore Peaks, wisps of mist sit for ever so long; intermingling a little and separating a little, they fool around with themselves trying to be born and become something. But when I get up and walk on they are still not finished.

I meet a line of ants, a procession of ants, of busy travelers. They do nothing and carry nothing, they just wander. I try to take a few steps back to see those at the head, to see their leader, but it's useless; I take more and more steps back, I begin to run, but the procession already stretches endlessly before and behind me. They may have started moving a week ago.

So I go my way, and the other ants go theirs, and so we all go.

Ah, but this place where I am now isn't really just a mountainside, no, it's a bosom, a lap, it's so soft. I climb up slowly, not trampling, not bearing down, I marvel at it: a big mountainside so tender and helpless, long-suffering as a mother, so that an ant can walk on it. If a half-overgrown stone lies here and there, it hasn't just fallen here, it belongs here, has lived here a long time. It's wonderful.

It's noon when I reach the height and look back. Far off on another mountainside is one of the cotters' cows, a quaint little cow with red and white sides; it just goes there. A raven sitting on a high crag tosses a remark my way, like an iron dip scraping against the crag. I feel a wave inside me and sense, as so many a time before in the open, that the place has just been deserted, that someone was here a moment ago and only stepped aside. Right now I'm standing here alone with someone, and a bit later I see a back disappearing into the forest. It's God, I think. There I stand without talking, without singing, just looking. I feel my whole face flooded with the sight. It was God, I think.

A vision, you say. No, a little insight into things, I reply. Do I make a god of nature? What about you?

Don't the Moslems have their god, the Jews theirs, the Indians theirs? No one knows God, my little friend, men know only gods. Now and then I seem to meet mine.

When I start home I head in a different direction, making a big detour. The sun is warmer now and the ground more rugged. I come to a big scree left by a landslide, and for fun I pretend I'm tired and throw myself down, just as if someone were watching me and seeing how fagged out I was. It's just for fun, and because my brain has been idle for so long, that I hit on this. The sky is completely clear, the wisps of mist over the Tore Peaks are gone, God knows where, but they have stolen away. Instead, an eagle floats in wide circles over the valley. Large and blackish and out of reach, it describes circle after circle up there, as though around an arena, eating its way slowly through the air, a thick-necked cock, an eagle stud surveying its territory. Oh, it's like a song to watch. Finally it disappears behind the peaks.

And here I lie, left behind with the scree and the little juniper bushes. How strange it all is! The stones in this rubble, maybe there is a meaning to them, they have lain here for thousands of years but maybe they travel too, going on indescribable journeys. The glaciers withdraw, the land rises, the land sinks, there is no hurry, it just happens. But since my mind doesn't connect anything with such an idea, it grows blind with anger and braces itself against it: the scree's migration doesn't exist, it's just words, a little joke. Well, then, the scree is a town, and all over the ground here and there lie parishes of stone. It's a peaceful community, no big events, no suicides, and there may be a well-formed soul in each of these stones. Still, God preserve me from some of the inhabitants of these towns, heh-heh: rolling stones. They can't bark, nor are they of interest to pickpockets, they are only dead weight. Well behaved, to be sure, but I do hold it against them that they display no fiery gestures, it would suit them to roll a little. But there they lie, no one even knows their sex exactly. On the other hand, did you see the eagle? You just be quiet. . . .

A breeze springs up. There are some ferns growing here — they bob a little — along with some flowers and blades of grass. But the grass can't bob, it only trembles.

Then I make my big detour and come down by the first cotter's place.

"In the end you, too, will probably build a health resort," I say in the course of our conversation.

"Oh no, we don't have the means for that, you know," he answers slyly. But in his innermost heart he probably wouldn't want to anyway, he has seen what it leads to.

I didn't like him, his eyes were servile and rested on the ground. The only thought in his head was about land; he had grown land-hungry, like an animal wanting to break out of its enclosure. The other cotter had bought a slightly larger piece of land than he, a bog that would feed one more cow; he himself had got only this parcel right here. "But maybe something can come of this too, as long as one has the health to keep working at it."

He grabbed his spade again.

XIII

At the table they talked about Solem. I don't know who started it, but some of the women thought he was good-looking; they nodded and said, "He's the right sort, all right!"

"What does it mean to say he's the right sort?" Master Høy asks, looking up from his dinner.

No one answers.

Then Høy can't help smiling and says, "Fancy that! I must take a look at Solem sometime, I really haven't taken notice of him before."

Høy could very well have a look at Solem, he

wouldn't grow any taller by it, nor Solem any shorter. But the good master was irritated, that was the crux. When a woman decides a man is the right sort, it's infectious, the other women get curious and stick out their beaks: "Oh, is he?" In a few days the whole flock is of the same opinion: "Oh yes, he's the right sort!"

Tough luck for all those humorless pedagogues!

Poor Master Høy — there sat even Mrs. Molie casting her nod for Solem. Frankly, she didn't seem to know much about it, but she wasn't going to let the others get an edge on her. "Mrs. Molie is nodding too," Høy said and smiled again. Oh, he was so annoyed. Then Mrs. Molie flushed and grew pretty.

By the next meal Master Høy couldn't help himself any longer and said, "Ladies, now my eyes have beheld Mr. Solem."

"Well?"

"A common burglar."

"Oh, shame on you!"

"You must at least admit he has a rather insolent face. Beardless. Blue chin, a horse's chin."

"There's no harm in that," Mrs. Molie said.

Well, listen to that! Mrs. Molie isn't quite out of circulation yet, I think to myself. Lately she also appeared to have a nice bit of padding on her bosom, so she no longer slouched as badly as before; she has also eaten and slept well — she has improved here at the resort. Oh sure, Mrs. Molie has still got some sparks in her.

In fact, this became apparent a few days later — poor Master Høy once again! For now we had a lawyer, a real go-getter, with us at the farm, and he talked more to Mrs. Molie than to anyone else. Had something come between her and Mr. Høy? True, he wasn't much to look at, but neither was she.

Well, the lawyer was a young sportsman and a go-getter, and he knew all about social science; he had also been to Switzerland and studied referendums. At first he had worked a couple of years for an architect, he said, but then he switched to law, which led in turn to social issues. He must have been a rich and dedicated man, to change careers so often and to travel so much. "Switzerland!" he said, his eyes watering. None of us could understand his great rapture.

"Yes, that must be an interesting country," Mrs. Molie remarked in response.

Master Høy looked ready to burst, he just couldn't restrain himself: "Speaking of Solem," he blurted out, "I've changed my mind about him in the last few days. He's ten times better than many others."

"Hear, hear!"

"Yes, he is. And he doesn't make himself out to be

more than he is. And what he is, he is with a vengeance. I saw him butcher the lame goat."

"You stood and watched?"

"I was just passing by. One, two, three, it was done. And later I saw him in the woodshed. He knows his work, that fellow. And I can well understand why women see something in him."

Look at Master Høy squirming! In the end he insists that skippers' wives whose husbands are on the China run must remain absolutely true to their Chinaman, they'd better be.

"Do be quiet a moment and let the lawyer tell us about Switzerland," Mrs. Molie said.

The artful witch, was she trying to push her fellow man, Høy, from the highest pinnacle of the Tore Peaks tonight?

But now Mrs. Brede spoke up. She seemed to understand Høy's anguish and wanted to help him. Hadn't the same Høy just uttered some friendly words about Solem, and wasn't Solem the lad who made her tear down her window shade one fine evening? Everything is connected.

"Switzerland," said Mrs. Brede in her gentle way, reddening and laughing a little, "I don't know anything about Switzerland; but I got some dress material from there once, and that was the worst swindle

I've ever come across."

The lawyer only smiled at this.

Miss Johnsen told us what she had learned about the watch factories and the Alps and Calvin — .

"Well, really, three things in a thousand years," Høy said, pale with suppressed anger, his face altogether changed.

"Have you gone mad, Master Høy?" Miss Palm exclaimed, laughing.

But the lawyer drew our admiration with his stories about Switzerland, that wonderful country, a model for all small nations of the world. Think of its social conditions, its referendums, its program for exploiting the country's natural resources; *there* were resorts, *there* they made an art of tourism! Superb!

"Yes, and its Swiss cheese," Høy said. "It reeks of tourists' feet."

Silence. So, Master Høy would stop at nothing!

"Well, what about Norwegian 'old cheese'?" said a friendly Danish voice.

"Yes, that's a damn nuisance too," Høy replied. "That's for our teacher, Mr. Staur, when he sits in his log chair."

Laughter.

But now things had been smoothed over a bit, and the lawyer could safely join in again: "If only we could make such Swiss cheese here at home," he said, "then we wouldn't be so poor. All in all, my bit of research around the country has convinced me that they are ahead of us in every respect. They can teach us everything, their thrift, diligence, working night shifts, cottage industries —"

"And so on!" Høy breaks in. "Trifles, nothings, nullity! A country that only exists by the grace of its neighbors ought not to be a model for any other country on earth. We must try to rise above that miserable thought, it only makes us petty. It's the great countries and the great things that should be our model. Everything grows, don't you see, even what is small, unless it's born to a Lilliputian existence. A child can of course learn from other children, but it models itself on adults. After all, the child will someday be grown, and what would happen if its model had always been an eternal child, a born Pygmy? That's what you're asking for with your Swiss twaddle. Tell me something: why, exactly, should we learn from the smallest and most insignificant countries?

"We're small enough already. Switzerland is Europe's cotter. Has anyone ever heard that the young South American countries of Norway's size take pride in becoming just like Switzerland? That's what makes Sweden forge ahead so wonderfully now; it doesn't look to Switzerland, it doesn't look to Norway, it looks to Germany. All honor to Sweden for that! And what about us? We shouldn't be just a small good-for-nothing people up among our Alps, producing peace conferences, skiing idols and Ibsen for a thousand years, we have the greatness in us to be a thousand times more — ."

The lawyer had been holding his hand up for a long time, to show he would like to answer, and now he shouted, "Just one word!"

Høy paused.

"Only one tiny little question, the smallest one can imagine," he said, preparing it carefully, "Have you ever set foot in the country you're talking about?"

"Yes, I have," Høy replied.

So! The lawyer gained nothing from his tiny little question. And now it came to light what a wicked thing Mrs. Molie really was: she'd known all along that Høy had been to Switzerland on a travel grant but never let on. Oh, the snake! On the contrary, she had encouraged the lawyer and no one else to tell stories from there.

"Oh yes, Master Høy has also been to Switzerland," she said, to smooth things over.

"In that case Master Høy and I have seen the country with different eyes, that's all," the lawyer said, wanting to leave it at that.

"They don't even have fairy tales," Høy said, finding it difficult to stop. "There they sit generation after generation filing watch wheels and guiding Englishmen up their peaks; but it's a country devoid of folk songs and fairy tales." Now we should work hard to make Norway the equal of Switzerland in this respect too, right?

"William Tell?" Miss Johnsen remarked, inquiringly.

Several women nodded, or at least Miss Palm did.

Then Mrs. Molie, turning her head to look out the window, said, "You certainly had a different opinion of Switzerland before, Master Høy."

That struck home. He wanted to answer, to finish her off, but thought better of it and kept silent.

"Don't you remember?" she asked, teasing him afresh.

"No," he replied. "You must have misunderstood me. Anyway, I don't see how, I think I'm quite understandable, I'm even used to explaining things to children."

That, too, struck home. Mrs. Molie didn't push it any further but smiled meekly.

"All I can say is that my opinion is the direct opposite of yours," the lawyer said once more. "However, I thought," he continued, "I thought this was something I had familiarized myself with, but —."

Mrs. Molie got up and went out, her head lowered as though she was about to cry. After sitting for a moment, Høy followed her. But he whistled and acted brave, as if he wasn't the least bit embarrassed.

"And what do you think?" Mrs. Brede asked the oldest person in the group, who happened to be me.

And as was proper for a man of mature years, I answered, "There may be some exaggeration on both sides."

With that everyone agreed. But to hell with compromising, I thought Høy was right. One has so many deplorably youthful opinions as long as one is still in the early seventies.

The lawyer finished as follows: "When all is said and done, it's Switzerland we have to thank for being able to enjoy this comfortable mountain retreat. We bring tourists into the country on the Swiss model, and make money to pay our mortgages. Ask the owner of this place if he would be willing to do without everything Switzerland has taught us. . . ."

In the evening Mrs. Brede asked, "Why did you make Master Høy so unreasonable today, Mrs. Molie?"

"Me?" said Mrs. Molie innocently. "You don't

think I —!"

It did seem, indeed, that Mrs. Molie had been innocent, for already the next morning she and Høy went quite merrily to the mountains together and were gone till noon. If there had been a scene, she had probably told her sorely tried friend something like this: "Believe me, I don't care anything about that lawyer, are you crazy! I only said a few words to him to make you polish him off, don't you see? Oh, you're the silliest, sweetest and — come over here and I'll kiss you. . . ."

XIV

After the big caravan, no more are coming. Some of us don't understand, others have a sort of hunch about what's wrong; but all of us are waiting — surely the travelers must come, we are the ones with the Tore Peaks!

But nobody comes.

The women at the farm do their daily chores for us and don't complain, but they aren't happy. Paul still takes it easy, sleeping a lot in the little room off the kitchen; but a couple of times at night I've seen him walking off toward the woods, deep in thought.

There were rumors from the neighboring valley that motorcars had now started operating there. That was the explanation for the slackness here with us! And one day a Dane came down from the mountain; he had scaled the Tore Peaks from the other side, which everyone had thought impossible till now. Sure, he'd just taken the motorcar to the foot of the mountains and then crossed over!

So now we didn't have the Tore Peaks anymore either!

I wonder if Paul shouldn't try and sow forage in his long field down by the river all the same. That was what he had intended to do at first anyway, but then the big caravan came and made him negligent. To be sure, it's now much too late in the year to sow anything, but with the field left as is there will be nothing but dock and chickweed. What if it were harrowed and sown? Why doesn't Paul think about such things instead of taking to the woods at night?

But Paul has lots of thoughts. His brain, that of a tiller of the soil, was at an early age diverted to the tourist trade, and there it got stuck. He hears that our hotshot of a lawyer is also an architect and asks him to draw up plans for the large new building, with six rooms, hall and bath; Paul has already ordered the log chairs and the reindeer antlers for the hall.

"If you weren't in this all by yourself, you too could get yourself some motorcars," the lawyer said.

"I've thought of that," Paul replied. "It's not impossible that I come up with something like that. But first I need the new building. And then I need a road."

The lawyer promised to design the building and went with him to look at the site. The project would cost so and so much; but Paul was already clearly aware of that, three or four good summers would pay for it. Paul saw no problems. As we walked about over there inspecting the site, I noticed he smelled of liquor.

Then a small party of Norwegians and foreigners showed up, hikers who came for the hiking, not to ride in a motorcar. The moment they came the spirits rose on the farm; the strangers stayed a few days, and Solem took them over the mountain and made good money. Paul himself was visibly encouraged, he put on his Sunday best and strutted about the property. He had a few things to talk over with the lawyer concerning the new building.

"If there's anything we should discuss, maybe we had better do it now," he said. "I'm going to be away for a few days."

They came to an agreement about a couple of small things relating to the building.

"Are you going to town?" the lawyer asked.

"No, just down to the village. I want to see if I can

get people to go along with some old ideas I've had: telephone and motor coach service and such."

"Good luck!" said the lawyer.

And so the lawyer sat there drawing up plans for the new building while the rest of us busied ourselves in our own way. Josephine went to Solem and said, "Go and sow that field down by the river, will you!"

"Did Paul say so?" he asked.

"Yes," she replied.

Solem went very reluctantly. As he was harrowing, Josephine came and said, "Harrow it one more time."

The clever little thing had more forethought than the men. She was so pretty as she bustled around; I often saw her with her hair messed up, but that didn't matter. And when she pretended that no one but the maids milked the goats and did the outdoor work, it was something she thought up for the sake of the house, its reputation. She must have learned to plunk the piano for the same reason. She was ably backed up by the mistress of the farm; the women were hard-working and thrifty, but Josephine was the one who was seen everywhere, being light as a feather. And what chaste little hands she had! I told her once, playing the wit, "Your name shall be Josephkin, because you are of the kin of Joseph!"

XV

Now Miss Torsen, our dark beauty, wanted to leave in earnest. She was healthy enough already, so she didn't need a sojourn in the mountains for that reason, and since she was bored here, why shouldn't she leave?

But a little incident made her decide to stay on.

In their extreme idleness the women at the resort occupied themselves with Solem. They had become so sated and so bursting with health that they needed to busy themselves with something, to have someone to fancy. And there was that lad Solem. More than once one of the women would come in to report what Solem had said and what Solem had thought, and they all pricked up their ears. Solem had become reckless and joked with the women, calling himself a man for all seasons; and once he had crassly bragged, "If you want to see a hellish fellow, look at me!"

"Can you guess what Solem just said?" Miss Palm asks. "He's chopping wood and has a rag on his finger that keeps getting stuck to the wood and bothering him, poor thing. Then Solem said, 'If only I could spare the time some day to cut off this damned finger!' he said."

"Tough, isn't he!" said the other women. "He's

capable of doing it."

A little later I walked by the woodshed and saw Mrs. Brede putting a new bandage on Solem's finger. . . . Poor woman, she was virtuous, but young.

It has been awfully hot during the day for some time now, the heat came in waves down the mountain and left us faint; but in the evening we regained some of our starch and did all sorts of things: some of us wrote letters or played forfeits outside, others were so refreshed that they went for a walk to "enjoy the scenery."

Sunday evening I was talking to Solem down by his room. He still had his Sunday clothes on and didn't seem to be going to bed.

Miss Torsen comes by, she stops and says to Solem, "I've heard you're going for a walk with Mrs. Brede."

Solem touches his cap, exposing a red line around his forehead from the sweatband.

"Who, me? Well, yes, she did hint at it. There was a path she wanted me to show her, she said."

Ah, Miss Torsen was really in the mood for devilry! Beautiful, desperate, she paced back and forth giving off sparks. Her little red felt hat was pinned to the back of her head and turned up high in front. Her throat was bare, and she was wearing a thin dress and low shoes.

Her behavior was altogether wonderful to watch as she opened a window to her secret. What did she care about Batt, that shopkeeper! Hadn't she drudged all her youth to get an education and then missed out on the substance? Poor Miss Torsen, Solem mustn't show another woman a new path this evening!

When nothing more happens and Solem is about to go, Miss Torsen clears her throat. She moves her lips and manages a smile — and there it sits, freezing up.

"Come with me instead!" she says.

Solem looks around quickly and answers, "Okay."

Then I left them, whistling and acting excessively nonchalant as I wandered off, as though nothing on earth concerned me anymore.

"Come with me instead!" she said. And they went. Now they are already behind the outhouses, now behind the two big rowan trees — they are hurrying so Mrs. Brede won't see them — now they're gone.

A door was wide open, but where did it lead? I saw no sweetness in her, only nervous excitement. She had learned grammar but no substance, her *nature* was undernourished. An upright girl, she should have married, she should have been a man's wife, a mother, a blessing to herself. How can she bring herself to snatch at a pleasure just to keep others from getting

85

it — she who is so tall and pretty!

A dog is guarding a bone. It waits until another dog has come close. Suddenly it seems to have a fit of ravenous appetite, grabs the bone with its teeth and crushes it. Because the other dog came by.

*

It looked as though this little incident was needed to prepare my mind for the night. I awoke in the dark and felt inside me this nursery rhyme I had fiddled with for so long, four singsong stanzas about the juniper bush.

Up on the steep mountainside
where the juniper bush takes root,
none of the other trees in the woods
are able to follow suit.
Little more than halfway up
the pine trees take to freezing,
a little higher — and the birches
go into fits of sneezing.
But an ever so little runt
is hearty and scrambles on,
there he is on top, the stunt,
standing barely two feet tall.
It looks as if he's driving

a lumber train to the valley.
That runt of a juniper bush
is now a regular jarvey.

In the valley there's summer lightning
and leafage and St. John's,
and there's song and children's games,
and now and then a dance.
Up here by the juniper bush
there is nothing to see but screes —
though sometimes you see a troll
lurking about on the prowl.
But the wind grabs the juniper bushes
and shakes their topmost bunches,
and the whole world lying around
is naked and, oh, so blustery.
But, ah, what freshness in the air!
There's nothing like it anywhere.
And nobody has as great a view
as juniper bushes do.

Over the mountain there hovers
a brief moment of summer,
and soon again the perpetual
shivering brr of winter!
But here is a juniper bush

with needles ever so green,
what a marvel of endurance
that the runt never gives in!
At last he becomes as strong
as the hardest bone and gristle,
with loads of berries when other trees
are naked, stripped to the skin,
and all the berries are marked
with a lovely cross on the chin.
So now we know this too,
what a juniper bush will do.

But once in a while he's likely
to hum somewhat like this:
Oh my, how here is lovely
and the sky, how blue it is!
And now and then he calls
to other juniper bushes
to pooh-pooh all those trolls
that prowl about the knolls!
Then the winter evening falls
on mountain and juniper holt,
and a thousand lights and stars
appear on the heavenly vault.
And then the juniper bushes
grow tired and, oh, so drowsy,

and soon one and all sleep tight.
And now good night, good night!

I straightened up, made a clean copy of my rhymes
and sent them to a certain little girl I'd taken many
walks with, and she learned them right away. Later I
read them to Mrs. Brede's little girls, and they stood
just like two bluebells, listening. Then they snatched
the papers out of my hand and ran to their mother
with them. They were so fond of their mother. And
she was fond of them too, they made a glorious racket
at bedtime.

Brave Mrs. Brede with her children! She could have
kicked up her heels, but didn't have the heart to do
so. Then she was probably rewarded for it. By whom?
By her husband?

A man should take his wife with him when he goes
to Iceland. Or take the consequences when she is left
to her fate at home for ever so long.

XVI

Miss Torsen didn't talk about leaving anymore. Not
that she looked particularly happy about staying either; but then Miss Torsen was altogether too restless
and odd to be satisfied with anything.

Of course she caught a cold that evening in the woods with Solem, and spent the next day in bed with a headache; but when she got up again there was nothing the matter with her.

Nothing? Why was her skin so blue under her chin, as if she had been grabbed?

She didn't cast a glance in Solem's direction anymore and acted like he didn't exist. So perhaps there had been a tussle in the woods, making her turn blue under her chin and causing them no longer to be friends? It would be just like her to be unwilling — wanting nothing but sensation, the triumph; and Solem hadn't understood anything and had flown into a rage. Was that it?

Sure, Solem seemed to have been cheated. He was more plain-spoken and less prudent, throwing out hints and saying things like, "That Miss Torsen, well, she's quite something, I bet she's as strong as a man!" Then he laughed, but his laughter was malicious. He followed her with dirty looks wherever she went, and to assert himself and pretend indifference he struck up a song from his lineman days when she was around. But he might as well have spared himself the trouble. Miss Torsen was stone-deaf to his song.

And now it looked as though she wanted to stay with us out of sheer spite. We had no more fun for

her than before, but she began to cozy up to the lawyer, sitting at his table in the common room when he
was working on the house plans. There is such a per-
verse idleness at mountain resorts.

*

And so the days pass; they have no novelty for me
any longer and I'm getting bored. Now and then a
stranger comes by, on his way over the mountain, but
it's not as in previous years, I'm told, when guests
came in droves. And it probably won't become any
better till we, too, get roads and motor coaches.

I haven't bothered to say it before, but the valley
beside ours is called Stordalen — Big Valley — while
ours is only called Reisa, after our river, and all of
Reisa is merely a parish-of-ease. So Stordalen has all
the advantages, even the name is grand. But Paul, our
host, calls the neighboring valley Vesledalen — Little
Valley — because the people there are so mean and
greedy, Paul says.

Poor Paul! He came back from his trip to the village just as hopeless as he went, and extremely drunk
to boot. He lay in his room for a day and more without coming out. When he finally reappeared he was
high and mighty, pretending he had accomplished a
great deal on his trip: they would find a way to pro-

vide motor coaches all right, never fear! But that same afternoon, after drinking again, he acted grand in a different way: bah, those poor devils down in the village didn't understand a thing, they hadn't been willing to help with a road to his place. He was the only one with a head on his shoulders. Wouldn't that bit of road be a blessing for the whole parish? For then, see, the caravans would come, showering money behind them through the whole valley. But they didn't understand a thing, those people.

"But sooner or later we must have a road here," the lawyer said.

"You bet!" Paul replied decisively.

Then he went inside and lay down in his room again.

But one day there came another small flock of visitors; having struggled with their baggage in the broiling-hot sun, they now wanted help with it. Solem was at once ready, but he couldn't possibly manage all their bags and cases, and Paul was lying in his room. I'd seen Paul going to the woods again the night before, talking aloud and gesticulating wildly as though someone were with him.

There stood the visitors.

The matron and Josephine came out and sent Solem over to Einar, the first cotter, to get him to help carry. Meanwhile the travelers got impatient and kept looking at their watches — if they didn't get over the Tore mountains in time they would have to spend the night outdoors. Someone suggested the delay might be deliberate, that the people here probably wanted them to spend the night; they started mumbling something to that effect, and eventually they asked, "Where's the man of the house, the proprietor?"

"He's sick," Josephine replied.

Solem came back and said, "Einar doesn't have time, he's weeding his potato patch."

Pause.

Then Josephine said, "I've got to be on the other side of the mountain anyway — wait a second!"

She was back in the blink of an eye, piled bags and cases on her little back and trudged off. The others followed.

I set off after Josephine and took her load. But I wouldn't let her turn back, this little outing away from the pension would do her good. We chatted a good deal as we went along: Josephine wasn't really in such a bad way, she had saved up quite a bit of money.

Once we had reached the mountain plateau, Josephine wanted again to turn back. She thought it was pointless just to go beside me, doing nothing but walking.

"But you were going to the other side anyway, weren't you?" I said.

She was too smart to deny it. For then the daughter at the time-honored Tore Peak resort would have come along just to carry bags for tourists. She answered, "Yes, but it's not urgent. I was to call on someone, but it can wait till winter."

We squabbled a bit about this, and I was ornery enough to threaten throwing the bags down the mountainside again, then she would see! "Then I'll just carry them myself, and *you* will see!" Josephine replied.

At that moment our group caught up with us. Before I knew it, one of the visitors grabbed the load off my back, doffed his cap and told me his own and the others' names, making a big fuss. I must pardon him, I must really forgive him, it was just too bad, he hadn't been thinking. . . .

If he only knew that I could easily have carried him on top of the bags! It's not strength that I lack, but day and night I'm carrying around the copycat of all diseases, and he's heavy as lead. Well, many another is groaning under a load of stupidity, that's no better. We each have our troubles. . . .

Then both Josephine and I turned to go home again.

*

Oh yes, I'm treated with a boundless politeness now, because of my age. People put up with me when I pester others, act eccentric, or have a screw loose; they forgive me because I've turned so gray. You with your pair of compasses will say, of course, that they are honoring me for the writing I've been doing for so long, but in that case I should have been appreciated when I was young and deserved it, not now when I no longer deserve it as much. No one — not a single one of us — can be expected to write nearly as well after fifty as before, it's only simpletons and self-servers who claim there's improvement after that age.

It's true, to be sure, that I've practiced a special kind of writing, and better than most; I know that very well. But I don't really have myself to thank for that, because I was born with the talent for it. That's a fact.

I have verified this, so I know it holds good. I've thought to myself: if only someone else had said this! Well, others have probably said it too at times, without it affecting me. But I've continued on, willfully exposing myself to outright literary disparagement by others without being affected by it. So I know what I'm talking about. On the other hand, my way of life has left me with an inner substance of importance, and for this substance I can certainly demand respect, it reflects some credit on me. Nobody can make me out to be an inferior person without playing false. But if you have an inner substance, you can endure even false play.

You can quote Carlyle against me — oh, how writers are mistreated: *Considering what book-writers do in the world, and what the world does with book-writers, I should say, it is the most anomalous thing the world at present has to show.* You can also cite many others, who will claim I'm now being lionized both for my writing, my inborn gift, and for my struggle to make it serviceable through self-discipline. And I claim only what's perfectly true: that the lionizing is mostly due to the fact that I've reached a venerable age.

This seems so wrong to me; such an attitude easily lends itself to spurning talent and shamelessly keeping the young down in favor of the old. Old age should not be revered for its own sake; it only delays and slows down the march of humankind. Indeed, primitive peoples despise age and rid themselves of it, and of the hindrance it represents, without any fuss. It was in the old days I deserved being lionized and would have appreciated it; now I'm better off in more than one sense and can do without.

But there it is. When I enter a room it falls respectfully silent. How he has aged! those present think. And they are silent so I can say something memorable in that room.

What quaint nonsense! The noise should rise to the rafters when I come in: Welcome, old boy, old comrade — but skip the memorable sayings, you should have given us those before, when you were better qualified. Sit down, old man, and keep us company. But don't block our light with your age, and don't hold us up; you had your time, now it's ours. . . .

There, that's honest talk.

In country homes they still have the right instinct: a mother will spare her daughters the coarse, simple work, and a father his son. A true mother will let her daughter sew while she herself goes to the cowshed. And, in turn, the daughter will do the same for her daughter. It's instinct.

XVII

Oh, it's getting more and more boring to be with people, I see nothing in them I haven't seen before. And so I settle for observing Solem's growing passion for Miss Torsen. But that too is familiar and boring.

Solem has become swell-headed from all the attention the women have bestowed on him. He has bought himself new clothes and a gilded watch-chain with the money he has earned; on Sundays he wears a sporty white woolen vest, though it's very warm, and his neck and chest are draped in an expensive silk tie with a sailor's knot. No one is as smart as he, and he knows it too — he sings as he crosses the yard and thinks no one too good for him anymore. Josephine will have none of his loud singing, but Solem is so indispensable to the place, he no longer obeys every order. He has his own way in many things now, even Paul himself takes a glass with him once in a while.

Miss Torsen seems to have settled down. She's very much attached to the lawyer and lets him explain every angle he draws in his house plan. She's quite right: the lawyer is no doubt her kind of man, a go-getter and a sportsman, wealthy, a bit of a simpleton, robust. At first Mrs. Molie seemed unwilling to put up with these two sitting together so much in the common room, she constantly found a pretext for going there. But what could Mrs. Molie be thinking of, with her ice-blue teeth?

Finally the lawyer had finished the plan and could hand it over. He again talked, as he had repeatedly before, about a certain peak among the Tore mountains that no one had yet scaled, it was just waiting for him. Miss Torsen was against the idea, and when she got to know the lawyer better, she begged him not to attempt such an insane climb. He smiled and promised to be good. They were in the fondest agreement.

Still, the blue peak stuck in the lawyer's mind; he pointed it out to Miss Torsen from the yard and smacked his lips, and his eyes watered again.

"God, I swoon just looking at it!" she said.

The lawyer supported her with his arm.

Solem winced at the sight; altogether his eyes popped out of his head when he saw the pair. One day as we came out from dinner he went straight up to Miss Torsen and asked, "I know another path, would you like me to show it to you tonight?"

There was some confusion, and Miss Torsen hesitated a little before she replied, "A path? No, thanks." She turned to the lawyer, saying as they left, "Whoever heard of such a thing!"

"What has come over him?" the lawyer said.

Solem went away, baring his teeth in a grin.

That evening Solem repeated the scene. He went again to Miss Torsen and said, "There's that path — should we go now?"

As soon as she saw him coming she quickly turned

around and tried to get away. But Solem shrank from nothing, he went after her.

"I'll tell you one thing," she answered, stopping: "If you get impertinent with me again I'll have you driven off...."

But it wasn't so easy to drive off Solem. He was a guide and porter for the tourists after all, as well as the only regular worker on the farm. And now that the haying was about to begin, he would have day laborers under him. No, Solem couldn't be driven off. Moreover, the other women seemed to stick by him; why, mighty Mrs. Brede alone could save Solem with a single word. She had the Tore Peak resort in her pocket.

As it turned out, nobody was fired; Solem kept himself in check from now on and became more civil. But he appeared to be as tormented as ever. One day around noon when he was alone in the woodshed, he made a slit in his thumbnail all the way across with the ax.

"What are you doing?" I asked.

"I'm just branding myself," he replied, laughing and giving me an ugly look. "When this slit has healed over, then —"

He paused.

"Then what?"

"Ah well, I'll probably be gone by then," he said.

But being left with the impression he had wanted to say something else, I tried to learn a little more.

"Let me see your finger. The cut is not deep, I guess you won't be here very long."

He mumbled, "Nails grow slowly, you know."

Then he went off whistling, and I set about chopping wood.

A short while later I saw Solem come back across the yard with a screeching hen under his arm. He went up to the kitchen window and asked, "Is this one of the hens you wanted?"

"Yes," he was told.

Solem came to the woodshed and asked for the ax, he was supposed to chop off the heads of some hens. Well, there you could see: he had to do everything, he was top dog and indispensable.

He put the hen on the block and took aim; but it wasn't an easy job, because the hen kept twisting her neck upward, like a snake, and refused to hold her head in place. She had stopped screeching now.

"I can feel her heart thumping wildly," Solem said.

Suddenly he saw his chance and struck a blow. There lay the head; Solem was still holding the body, it quivered in his hand. The whole thing happened so fast that, to my eyes, the two parts of the fowl were still one; a separation so absurd, so mad, conveyed nothing to me. It was a second or two before my eyes caught up with the event. The bewilderment was manifest in the expression of the separated head; it looked as if it didn't believe the whole thing, raising itself a little to show that nothing was the matter. Then Solem let the hen go. She lay still a moment, then gave a kick, got off the ground and started to flap her wings, the headless body lurching on one wing into the wall and spattering blood all around before lying still.

"I let her go too soon, after all," Solem said.

Then he went to get another hen.

XVIII

I come back to the wild idea of firing Solem. True enough, a certain disaster here at the resort would probably have been averted that way, but who would then have been top dog for us? Paul? But he was lying in his room, as I've said, lying there more and more; he never showed himself to his guests except by some erroneous maneuver on his part.

One evening he crossed the yard. In his confusion about the time he probably thought the guests had already gone to bed, but we were sitting outside, because it was dark and mild. When Paul became aware of this, he straightened up and said hello in passing, called Solem over to him and said, "You're not to take such trips over the mountain anymore without notifying me first. I was in my room, you know, I was writing. To have Josephine carry bags, whoever heard the likes!"

Paul walked on. But he still hadn't been grand enough, so he turned around and asked, "Why didn't you take along one of the cotters to help?"

"They refused," Solem replied, "they were weeding their potatoes."

"They refused?"

"Einar said no."

Paul thought it over.

"Acting like big shots, eh? They'd better not go too far; if they do, I'll drive them off their plots."

That roused the lawyer's legal instinct and he asked, "Haven't they bought their plots?"

"Oh yes," Paul replied. "But it's me, after all, who still lives on this farm. That should mean something, don't you think? Heh-heh-heh. I suggest to you I still have a bit of influence here in Reisa, heh-heh-heh. . . ." Then he grew serious and told Solem straight out, "Next time you let me know."

And with that he headed for the woods again.

"He's hitting the bottle now, good old Paul," the lawyer said.

No one replied.

"What if the manager of a resort in Switzerland went around like that!" he then said.

Mrs. Brede answered quietly, "It's a shame. He never used to drink."

The lawyer was immediately amiable again. "I'll have a nice little talk with him about it," he said.

*

But now there came a time when Paul was sober from morning till night: Brede, the merchant, arrived. The flag went up, there was a big hoopla, Josephine's feet said "brr" under her skirt. Mr. Brede came with a porter, his wife and children met him way up the road; the personnel also went to meet him.

"Hello!" he greeted us, making a big flourish with his hat and finding favor with us all.

He was big and friendly, stout, jovial, with the expansive cheerfulness that wealth brings. He was immediately our good friend.

"How long will you stay, Papa?" asked his little girls, hanging on to him.

"Three days."

"That's all!" his wife said.

"That's all?" he answered, laughing. "That's not so little, my friend, three days is a lot for me."

"But not for me and the children," she said.

"Anyway, a full three days. Let me tell you something: I've had to be pretty active to be this passive, ha-ha-ha."

In we went, the merchant had been here before and knew the way to his wife's cottage. He ordered some seltzer water right away.

That evening after the girls had gone to bed, the merchant and his wife joined us in the common room. He had whiskey with him for the gentlemen and ordered seltzer; for the ladies he had wine. It turned into a little party — the merchant was a practiced host, we were all very pleased. This portly man grew quiet and soft when Miss Palm played folk tunes on the piano, and he was no lazybones who sat around thinking only of himself; all of a sudden he would run out and take down the flag. "A flag should be lowered at sunset," he said. He also went to check whether the girls were sleeping a couple of times. All in all the children were very dear to him; he had factories and resorts and much more, but he seemed to be most proud of having children.

Someone from Bergen tapped his glass and began to speak.

The folks from Bergen had been so quiet, burring their r's in all modesty; but here was an all too tempting occasion to make speeches. Did we not have a visitor with us from the great, bustling world out there, bringing wine and joy and celebration? Rare commodities up here, in our blue, stony fastness. . . . And so forth.

He talked on for five minutes, getting better and better at it.

The merchant told us a little about Iceland — a neutral country neither Master Høy nor the lawyer had visited and therefore couldn't disagree over. One of the Danes had been there and could only confirm the correctness of the merchant's impressions.

But mostly he told little jokes.

"I have a servant, a young lad; one day when I was mad he said to me, 'You've become much better at cursing in Icelandic!' Ha-ha-ha, he gave me credit: 'You've become much better at cursing in Icelandic,' he said."

Everyone laughed, and his wife asked, "What did you say?"

"What I said! I was disarmed, ha-ha-ha."

Then someone else from Bergen spoke: Didn't we have the family of the man from the great bustling world with us, his wife, "a peerless lady spreading charm all around," and his children, those cavorting butterflies! . . . And several minutes later, "A glorious long life!"

He played a flourish on the piano.

The merchant drank a toast with his wife. "That's that," he said.

Mrs. Molie sat over in a corner talking louder and louder to the Dane who had crossed the Tore Peaks from the wrong side; she seemed to talk loudly on purpose. Taking notice, the merchant wanted to know more about the motor coaches in the neighboring valley, how many there were, how fast they went; the Dane gave him the information.

"Just imagine, crossing the mountain to get here!" said Mrs. Molie. "That's never been done before."

Prompted by the merchant, the Dane also told us about his adventurous expedition.

"There's supposed to be a blue peak up there somewhere," said Mrs. Molie, "that must be next, eh? Won't you ever stop?"

Well, the Dane was sorely tempted by that peak, but he said it probably couldn't be done.

"I would have scaled that peak long ago if you hadn't forbidden me, Miss Torsen," the lawyer said.

"I don't believe you could have," Mrs. Molie remarked nonchalantly. Her revenge, no doubt. She

107

turned again to the Dane, as though she expected great things from him.

"I forbid each and every one of you to think about that peak," put in Miss Torsen. "It's as naked as a ship's mast."

"What if I had a go at it, Gerda?" the merchant asked, smiling at his wife. "I'm an old sailor, after all."

"You, indeed!" she said, chuckling.

"I went aloft in a schooner last spring."

"Where?"

"Off Iceland."

"Whatever for?"

"However, I don't know — I can't figure out this mountain climbing business," the merchant said.

"But whatever for, can't you hear! Why did you go aloft?" his wife repeated nervously.

The merchant laughed. "Oh, the fair sex is really the most curious sex on earth!"

"How can you do such things? What about the girls and me, if you had —"

She said nothing more. Her husband turned serious and took her hand.

"There was a storm, my friend, the sails were flapping, it was a matter of life and death. But it was wrong of me to mention it. Well — I think we'll take our leave now, Gerda."

The merchant and his wife stood up.

Then the first fellow from Bergen again began speaking.

*

The merchant stayed with us his three days and was now ready to leave. He was always the same, contented and amusing. A bottle of seltzer was brought to him every evening, no more, and he and the little girls made a terrible racket at bedtime. But during the night there came a mighty snoring from his house. The girls had previously spent a good deal of time with me, now I didn't exist, being so taken up with their father. He made a swing for them between the two rowan trees off in the field, and wound plenty of rags under the rope so it wouldn't chafe the branches.

He did have a conversation with Paul; there were rumors that the merchant was withdrawing his investments in the Tore Peak resort. Paul walked with a stoop now, but what seemed to offend him the most was that the merchant also dropped by at the cotters', to see how they were doing. "He went over there?" Paul said. "Well, then, let him stay there!"

The merchant joked to the very end. He too may have been a bit saddened by the leave-taking, but he had to keep the others in check. Mrs. Brede was clutching his arm with both of hers, and the children were hanging on to the other — the picture of a family.

"I can't wave to you," the merchant said, laughing. "They won't let me say goodbye."

The girls rejoiced at this and shouted that, no, they wouldn't give him back his arm. "Hold tight you too, Mama!"

"Hush!" their father said. "I'm going to Scotland, just a short trip, you see. And when you get back from the mountains I'll be home too."

"Scotland? What are you going to Scotland for again?" the children asked.

The merchant turned and nodded to us, "Listen to the fair sex, nothing but curiosity!"

But his family didn't laugh.

He went on, talking to us, "By the way, I recently told my wife about a man who also was curious: he shot himself just to find out what came after life. Ha-ha-ha. That must be the very pinnacle of curiosity, don't you think? To shoot oneself just to find out about the afterlife!"

But he wasn't able to cheer his family up even with this. His wife stood still, her face was so pretty.

"So you're leaving now, are you?" she simply said.

There came the merchant's porter with his luggage; he had stayed over these few days, waiting.

And so the merchant took leave of the farm, followed down the field by his wife and children.

*

I don't know — this man with his high spirits and
good humor and wealth and all, sweet to his children,
everything for his wife —
Was he also everything *to* his wife?
He wasted the first evening partying, he wasted
time every night snoring. And thus the three days
passed. . . .

XIX

During the haying it's much more fun here. Scythes
are being whetted out in the fields, men and women
are at work, going about lightly dressed and bareheaded and calling back and forth to one another
and laughing; from time to time they drink from a
bucket of whey and then set to work again. And there
is the right fragrance from the hay, it penetrates my
senses like a tune from home, calling me home, home,
though I'm not abroad. Then I must be abroad all
the same, I think, separated from my own soil.
Why am I still here anyway, at a resort with
schoolmarms and a host who once again has said

farewell to all sobriety? Nothing happens to me, I'm nobody here. The others go out and lie down on their backs, I sneak away and savor myself and feel verses shaping up for the night — that makes it even. The world doesn't need verses, it only needs verses that haven't been sung before.

And Norway doesn't need any great red irons; it's the village blacksmiths that do the forging now, to the crowd's requirements and the country's glory.

*

No tourists came; a stream of them flowed up and down Stordalen, leaving our little Reisadalen empty. But what if the Nordland rail extension would come someday, bringing Bennett's and Cook's caravans up into Reisa — then Stordalen would wither in turn. Cotters wanting to farm will doubtless get to mow the freeholders' outlying meadows for an even share of the yield down through the ages, you bet they will. There is a good chance of that. Unless our descendants are wiser than we are and no longer let themselves be infected by the demoralization of the tourist trade.

But you don't have to take it from me, my little friend, you can just shake your head. A certain professor is cracking jokes around the country, a born mediocrity with a little knowledge of history from schoolbooks — ask him. He will give you exactly as much general information as you can take in and your brain can stand, my little friend.

*

No sooner had the merchant left than Paul began living a most irregular life once more. Things seemed to be closing in on him more and more on every side, and seeing no way out he made himself blind, which he then used as an excuse for not seeing. Now seven of our regular guests left us at the same time: the telephone operators, Mr. Batt, Miss Johnsen and Miss Palm, and two gentlemen engaged in trade, I'm not quite sure what kind. The whole flock crossed the mountain to be able to ride a motor coach in Stordalen.

Crates of various foodstuffs arrived for Paul, they were brought up one evening by a man from the village. The road being what it was, he'd had to take the sides off his cart and make several trips, carrying the crates one by one over the worst spots. Josephine received all the merchandise, and when she came to a crate that sloshed, she said it had been misdelivered. She wrote a new address on it and told the man to take it back; it was fruit juice that came too late, she said, she had already gotten juice from somewhere else.

Later that evening word spread from the kitchen that the crate was being discussed: the juice was not late, Paul said, losing his temper. "And take away these newspapers, why don't you!" he yelled. Then we heard paper and glass being swept to the floor.

Oh well, it wasn't so easy to be Paul either; his days were empty and dull, and he had no children the thought of which could give him a bit of cheer now and then. And while wanting to put up more buildings, he didn't need half of those he already had. Mrs. Brede and her children had a house to themselves, and after the seven guests were gone, Miss Torsen had the whole South Building to herself as well. Paul wanted to build a road, he wanted to keep pace with the growing tourist industry to his last breath and begin with motor coaches; but since he hadn't himself the means for this and didn't get any help, he could do nothing but submit. And now the merchant, Mr. Brede, had withdrawn his money. . . .

Paul stuck his careworn face out the kitchen door. He probably wanted to see if it was safe in the yard, but it wasn't; the lawyer called, "Good evening, Paul!" and dragged him out.

The two of them walked down the field in the twilight.

Not that it is any use to "talk" to a man about reducing his thirst, telling him that vital interests are at stake. But Paul must have agreed with every word the lawyer uttered, and he no doubt went away with good intentions.

Paul went to the village again. He was going to the post office to send some of the money left behind by those seven guests to the four corners of the world. It didn't cover everything, it didn't cover anything — not interest and repayment on loans, not taxes, not building maintenance — nothing but some crates of foodstuffs from town. Well, he did manage to stop that crate of juice from being sent back.

Paul came home blind drunk, he didn't want to see anymore. It was the same all over again. But all along his brain seemed to be working in a fashion to find a remedy. One day he asked the lawyer, "What do you call those glass boxes with little fish, goldfish, in them?"

"You mean aquariums?"

"Maybe that's it," Paul said. "Are they expensive?"

"I don't know. Why?"

"I wonder if I shouldn't get one of them."

"What do you want with that?"

"So you don't think it would attract any tourists? No? Well, I guess not."

And Paul withdrew.

More and more nonsense. Some see flies, Paul saw goldfish.

XX

The lawyer is constantly keeping company with Miss Torsen, he even pushes her in the children's swing and slips his arm around her to steady her when she wants to stop. Solem is observing this from the hayfield and begins singing a smutty song. He seemed to feel so wronged by those two; if he was ever to sing lewdly in self-defense, now was the time to do it, everybody would surely agree with him in that. That's why he sang so terribly loud, ending with a holler, "Yippie!"

But Miss Torsen swings and swings, and the lawyer slips his arm around her and stops her more than once. . . .

It's Saturday night. I'm talking to the lawyer in the yard; he's unhappy and wants to leave, but Miss Torsen won't go with him, and going alone is a bore. He doesn't hide his intimacy with her.

Solem comes along, he tips his cap and says hello. Then he glances around quickly and starts talking to the lawyer, politely, only as a menial.

"The Dane wants to climb that peak tomorrow. I'm supposed to bring a rope and go with him."

The lawyer jumps up. "Supposed to —?"

It was strange to watch the lawyer, he looked blank. His little sporting brain snapped. It lasted but a moment.

"Yes, tomorrow morning," Solem said. "I wanted to let you know. Because it was you who mentioned it first."

"Yes, that's true," the lawyer said, "I did indeed. And now he's beating me to it."

Solem knew how to remedy that. "Well, I didn't give him a definite answer," he said. "I told him I'd planned to go down to the village tomorrow."

"But we can't very well fool him either. No, that I won't."

"How annoying," Solem said. "Everyone says the first one up Blue Peak will be in the papers."

"He's sure to get terribly sore," the lawyer mumbled, thinking it over.

But Solem kept at it. "I don't think so. And besides, you mentioned it first."

"Everyone here will know, I won't even get permission," the lawyer said.

"We'll go at daybreak," Solem replied.

Eventually they came to an agreement.

"You won't tell anyone, will you?" the lawyer said to me.

*

People were asking about the lawyer all morning, he wasn't in his room, he wasn't in the yard. "Maybe the Danish mountain climber knows something," I said. But it turned out that the Dane hadn't talked to Solem at all about scaling Blue Peak today. He knew nothing about the expedition.

I was greatly surprised.

I looked at my watch, it was eleven. I had kept an eye on the peak since I got up, but without finding out anything with the help of my field glasses. By now it must have been five hours since the two headed for the mountains.

At half-past eleven Solem came running home, he was wringing wet with perspiration and hadn't spared himself.

"Come and help!" he shouted pointlessly to us as we stood around him.

"What's wrong?" someone asked.

"He fell!"

How Solem heaved and sweated! But what could we do to help? Run up into the mountains and see the accident for ourselves?

"Can't he walk?" someone asked.

"He's dead," Solem said. He looked from one to another of us, as if trying to make out whether his message was believable. "He fell, he didn't want me to help him."

A few more questions and answers, and there was Josephine on her way across the field already, she was going to the village to telephone for the doctor.

"We have to get him back here," said the Danish climber.

He and I started nailing together a stretcher; Solem got some brandy and rags and headed back up the mountain, followed by the men from Bergen, Mr. Høy, Miss Torsen, and Mrs. Molie.

I asked the Dane, "You really didn't talk to Solem about climbing that peak today?"

And he answered, "No, I didn't say a word to him about it. And if I were to climb it, I certainly wouldn't bring any company."

Later that afternoon we brought the lawyer back on the stretcher. Solem was explaining all along how the accident had happened; he repeated what he'd said and what the lawyer had answered, pointing to landmarks along the road — as if this stone over here were the lawyer and over there was the bottomless abyss. . . . Solem was still carrying the rope he'd had no use for in his hand. Miss Torsen asked no more questions than the rest and uttered only commonplaces: "I warned him against it, I asked him nicely to forget about it."

For all our talk, the lawyer was gone. It was so strange: his watch was running, but he himself was dead. The doctor could do nothing here, he went straight back to the village.

It was a difficult evening. Solem went to telegraph the lawyer's family in town, and the rest of us did what seemed most decent, sitting over our books in the common room. Now and then someone alluded to the accident: there you could see what we mortals were! Master Høy, himself a non-tourist, was very apprehensive that the disaster would hurt the resort and make it even harder for Paul: people would be likely to shun a place where they fell to their deaths.

No, Høy was no tourist, he didn't know the Anglo-Saxons.

Paul himself seemed to have an inkling that the disaster might not hurt him, he put a bottle of cognac on the table to comfort us on this sad evening.

And since we owed this courtesy to a death, one of the folks from Bergen launched into a speech.

XXI

The accident became widely known. Journalists came from town, and Solem had to go with them up into the mountains and show them death. If the body hadn't been taken away at once, they would have written about that too.

Children and shallow people might think it was wrong to snatch Solem away from the haying and everything else in field and meadow; but shouldn't business, the resort's business, come first? "Solem, here are some tourists!" they shouted to him from the yard. And Solem dropped his work. He was besieged by hosts of journalists who grilled him and dragged him to the mountains, to the scene of the accident; there was a saying about the place, heard each time Solem was missing: Solem is with death.

But Solem was not with death at all, he was with life, bright and shining, he feasted and flourished. Once again he was an important personage, sought out and listened to by strangers. And not just by women, no indeed — and this was something new, a change — by smart, eager gentlemen from town.

To me, Solem said, "Isn't it odd that the accident happened just when that cut in my finger had healed?" He showed me his thumb, that there was no mark on it anymore.

And the journalists telegraphed and wrote, not only about Blue Peak and violent death, but about the whole place, the Tore Peak health resort, a haven for the weary, with its magnificent buildings like jewels in a mountain setting. What a surprise to come here — gargoyles, a room with a fireplace, piano, all the newest literature on the tables, lumber outside for yet more jewels in a mountain setting, all in all a splendid portrait of modern Norwegian agriculture.

Oh sure, the journalists understood. And they did their bit of puffery.

Then the Anglo-Saxons came.

"Where's Solem?" they said. "Where's Blue Peak?" they said.

"We ought to get the hay in too," Josephine and the farmer's wife said, "it'll rain, and fifty loads are still out!" "That's all right, but where's Solem?" asked the Anglo-Saxons. And Solem had to come forward. The two hired hands started carting hay, but that left the women shorthanded with the raking and confusion reigned. One and all scurried in every direction, because there was no one to give orders.

But the weather held overnight, it was a long-suffering weather. If only the dew were gone, then more hay could be brought in, maybe all of it. Oh, it would be all right.

Then came more Anglo-Saxons. "Solem? Blue Peak?" they said. Their perverted sportsman's brains prickled and itched, they had carefully slipped by every insane asylum along their way and come straight here without being apprehended. And there stands Blue Peak, a ship's mast against the sky, ah! They rushed off, Solem could barely keep up with them; they would sink into the ground with shame if they didn't get to stand on this remarkable scene of an accident, this splendid abyss. Some would scale Blue Peak or never know another happy day in their lives, others would only get a sexual thrill from the lawyer's fatal fall; they would send down a yawp and wait for an echo, standing so close to the edge that they stepped on death with their toes. "Hurry up, Solem!"

But it is an ill wind that blows nobody any good: the resort made precious money. Paul revived again, and his face lost its wrinkles. A man who is good for something grows enterprising when he prospers, when there are setbacks he faces them out. A man who won't stand up to adversity is no good, let him go under! Paul wasn't drinking anymore, he even took an interest in the haying and started giving a hand in the field in Solem's place. If he had just been there earlier when the weather was long-suffering! But in any case

Paul started over from the right end; now he regretted having farmed out to his cotters those outlying meadows they were used to harvesting for an even share of the hay, he would have wanted them himself this year. But he'd given his word already, there was nothing to be done about that.

And besides it was raining. They couldn't go on gathering in the hay, they even had to stop cocking it. Enough hay to winter three cows was still out.

*

It didn't take long before the novelty wore off the Tore Peak resort again. The journalists telegraphed and wrote about other lovely accidents, and the death on Blue Peak was no longer a big deal. It had been a drunken binge, now came the morning after.

The Danish mountain climber simply gave up. He laced up his rucksack and walked over the mountain like anyone else, without bothering with Blue Peak. All the craziness he'd witnessed in the last week had taught him to be sensible.

And the stream of tourists flowed to other places.

What did I do to them, Paul must have thought, since they are staying away again? Did I spend too much time in the field and too little at home with them? But I did greet them humbly and even took my hired man away from the farmwork to wait on them. . . .

Then came two youths; sportsmen to their fingertips, they talked about nothing but sailing, cycling, and soccer — they were Norwegian hopefuls, engineers in the making: Young Norway. They too wanted to climb Blue Peak, doing their humble best; they had to keep up with progress, after all. Ah, but they were so young, they got scared when they stood at the foot of the peak, looking up. But Solem, that good lad, had learned more than one trick in dealing with tourists: he thoroughly soaked the two budding sportsmen, getting paid off not to blab about their cowardice. Then all was well, and the young hopefuls came down again, swaggering in front of us to show they had the right sportsman's stuff in them. One had brought with him from the mountain a bloodstained rag, which he flung down with the words, "There's the rest of that lawyer of yours who fell down!"

"Ha-ha-ha-ha!" the other young hopeful laughed.

They had learned such dashing bravery in sporting circles.

*

It rained for three weeks, then came two days without rain, and then it rained again for two weeks. The sun was nowhere to be seen, the sky was invisible, the peaks were also gone, we could see only rain. And already several roofs were leaking at the Tore Peak farm.

The hay that still lay spread in the fields turned black and rotted, and the cocked hay fermented and became worthless.

The cotters had gotten their hay in during the long-suffering weather. They carried it in on their backs, husband and wife and children.

The folks from Bergen and Mrs. Brede with her children have left. The little girls curtsied and thanked me for taking them for walks among the crags and telling them stories. Then they left. The resort is empty now, Master Høy and Mrs. Molie were the last ones; they left us last week, going their separate ways, though they were headed for the same small town — he went to the village and took a long roundabout way, she went over the mountain. It's very quiet here now, but Miss Torsen is still around.

Why don't I leave? I don't know. Why ask? Here I am, that's all. Have you heard anybody ask, How much does a northern light cost? Keep quiet!

And where would I go if I left? Maybe you think I want to go back to the city again? Or that I yearn for my turf hut and the winter and Madame? I yearn for nowhere, I just yearn.

Of course, I should be old enough by now to understand what every bright Norwegian understands, namely, that our country is heading in the right direction. Look, you can read in the papers about the wonderful progress made by tourism in Stordalen since the opening of the motor coach run. So, why shouldn't I go there and rejoice?

By force of habit I'm still here, interested in the few of us who remain. Miss Torsen is here.

Miss Torsen, what more is there to be said about her? What indeed! But she isn't leaving, she's still around, completing the portrait of her type: the middle-class child reared on nothing but schoolbooks growing up, who has learned about *Artemis cotula* but starved her own nature. That's what she's doing here.

I remember how a few weeks ago, at the time of the Anglo-Saxons, a young hopeful came down from the mountain with a bloodstained rag, tossed it on the ground and said, "There's the rest of that lawyer of yours who fell down!" Miss Torsen heard it without moving a muscle. No, the lawyer's accident didn't weigh on her for a moment; on the contrary, she wrote at once to summon another friend. When he appeared he turned out to be a flashy madcap — an "isolated figure," as he called himself in the visitors' book. I haven't mentioned him before because he was less important than she was, less important than any of us, in fact. He was beardless and V-necked, Lord knows whether he wasn't associated with some theater or cinema. Miss Torsen went to meet him when he came, bid him welcome and thanked him for coming, so she must have written and asked him to come. But why didn't she just go away? Why was she getting stuck in this place, even making others come here? She who had been the first to talk about leaving us this summer! There must be something behind it.

XXII

On reflection I understand that her not leaving has to do with Miss Torsen's love life; what's behind it is that this fellow Solem is still around. How odd — and how warped this beautiful young woman was! Lately I'd seen her, tall and proud, upright and untouched, stride deliberately close to Solem without acknowledging his greeting. Did she suspect he was involved in the lawyer's death and did she shun him on that account? Not at all; she shunned him less than before, she would even let him take her letters to the post office, which she hadn't done previously. Oh, she was so unbalanced, a poor soul gone astray. Whenever she had a chance, she would muck around on the sly with tar, and with dung in the field, sniffing at the filth without getting nauseated.

One day when Solem swore a needlessly coarse oath at a horse that wouldn't stand still, she glanced at him, trembled and turned crimson. But she checked herself at once and asked Josephine, "Isn't that man going to leave soon?"

"Yes," Josephine replied, "in a few days."

Though Miss Torsen had taken this opportunity to ask her question casually, it was no doubt important to her. She walked away without another word.

Oh no, Miss Torsen did not leave, she was sexually bound to Solem. Solem's desperation, Solem's coarse passion that she herself had kindled, his brutality, his maleness, his grasping hands, the way he looked at her — she sniffed at all this and felt something stir inside her. She had been led so astray, been so unnaturally damaged, that her desire was satisfied by the mere thought of this man at a certain distance from her. I suspect that, as she lay in her lonely bed in the evening, the Torsen type was taking delight in the fact that, in an entirely different building, a man lay writhing with lust for her.

But what about her friend, the actor? He was in no

way a match for Solem. There was no aurochs in him, no action, only theatrical swagger. . . .

*

Oh well, life is again making me petty and small, and I ask Solem about that old accident. We are alone in the woodshed.

Why had he lied and said that the Dane was going to scale Blue Peak that fateful Sunday?

Solem looked at me, he understood nothing.

I asked again.

Solem denied having said a word about it.

"I stood and heard you," I said.

"No, you didn't," he said.

Pause.

Then he fell on his face in the shed and lay crumpled up, all of a heap, just taking up space, and it took awhile before he was on his legs again. When he'd gotten up we looked at each other as he straightened his clothes. I didn't feel like talking to him anymore and just left him standing there. He would be leaving soon anyway.

After that there was nothing but boredom and emptiness again, and to mimic myself I go to a place apart and shout, "Bricks for the castle! The calf is much healthier today!" And after that I did other nothings, and when my money started to run out I wrote to my publisher, holding out the prospect of soon sending him an incredibly interesting manuscript. In short, I acted like someone who was in love. All the symptoms were there.

To take the bull by the horns: you probably suspect me of dwelling on Miss Torsen out of self-interest? If so, I believe having carefully hidden, in these pages, the fact that I never think of her except as an object, a topic; just turn back the pages and see! At my age one doesn't fall in love without becoming grotesque, without making the pharaohs laugh.

Done with that.

But one thing I'll never be done with: withdrawing to sit in the solitude of my room, surrounded by a deep darkness. In spite of all, that's the last joy.

*

An interlude.

Miss Torsen and her actor come walking, I can hear their footsteps and their talk. But since it's dark in the evening where I sit, I cannot see them. They stop outside my open window, leaning against it, and the actor is talking; he's asking her to do something she doesn't want, trying to pull her along with him, but she resists.

Then he loses his temper. "Why the hell did you write for me then?" he asks angrily.

She starts crying and says, "So that's the only reason you came, oo-oo! But I'm not at all like that, just leave me alone, I'm not doing you any harm."

And I'm supposed to understand women! Sheer conceit, brag. At this point I intervened, her crying sounded so terrible. I moved my chair and cleared my throat to let them know I was there.

He noticed immediately, shushed her and wanted to listen, but she said, "It's nothing. . . ."

It wasn't nothing, of course, and she knew it. But it was not the first time Miss Torsen used this trick with me, she had pretended before that she was out of earshot and then staged some choice scene. And each time I had promised myself not to interfere. But she hadn't cried before, this time she did.

Why did she perform these tricks? To clear herself in my eyes, in the eyes of a man of mature years, and show that she was good, that she was behaving properly? But dear child, I knew that already, I could tell from your hands! Your nature is so warped that here you are in your twenty-seventh year and unmarried, barren and unopened!

The pair went away.

*

And there is another thing I'll never be done with: withdrawing to sit in the solitude of the forest, surrounded by a deep darkness. That's the last joy.

It's the lofty, religious aspect of solitude and darkness that makes us need them. On the other hand, we do not seek to get away from others simply because we can only endure ourselves, oh no. The mystery is that everything surges toward us from afar, but everything is near, we sit in the midst of an omnipresence. I suppose it's God. I suppose it is one's self as a part of the all.

My heart wants what, my foot goes where?
Shall the forest be left to its fate?
There was my home, my abandoned lair.
I stop on my walk toward town, aware
that the night is passing, it's late.

The sleeping world that I survey
rings silent and sweet in my ear.
The paved-over city, big and gray,
is where all others go to stay,
but what shall I do, oh dear!

Ding-dong? Bells ringing in the barrow?

I turn around in the midnight gloom
to the woodland peace so deep.
I know of a bird-cherry full of perfume,
I'll go lay my head amid heather bloom,
and the forest will lull me to sleep.

Ding dong! Bells are ringing in the barrow.

Romantic? Sure. Only sentimentality and feeling
and verse, nothing? Sure.

That's the last joy.

XXIII

The sun is coming out. It doesn't come darkly glow-
ing and regal, it's imperial, because it sputters. My
little friend, you won't understand this, no matter what
slipshod language you hear these days. But right now
there is an imperial sun in the sky.

It's a good day for taking to the woods, it's mush-
room season, those yellow creatures are suddenly there.
They weren't there a short while ago, or I didn't see
them, or they were the color of the earth. There is
something unborn about them, they resemble fetuses
at an early stage; but if I turn them around they are
miracles of completion.

Here are milk caps, champignons, puffballs. Here's death cap, and goodness how it stands there, a member of the dear champignon family, looking innocent yet being pernicious! Have you ever seen such terrible cunning? A noxious fruit, criminal, showy, brilliant, but the epitome of professional viciousness, the cardinal of mushrooms. I break off a piece and chew it, it feels nice and soft on the tongue, but since I'm a coward I spit it out again. Wasn't it the death cap that made berserkers out of the Vikings? But at the dawn of our age we die of a hair in the throat.

The sun is already sinking. The cattle are grazing far off in the hills, but now they are coming home. I can hear by their bells that they are on their way. Thin bells and deep bells, sometimes they tinkle together so that it makes sense, a chord. It's so nice.

And it's also nice to look at the grass, the little wildflowers and the plants. There is a small legume where I'm lying, it is so strangely quiet, a few seeds are sticking out of it — dear God, it's about to become a mother. It has gotten tangled with a dry twig and I release it. Life pulses through it, the sun finally warmed it today and called it to its destiny. Look at that little tremendous miracle!

Now it's sundown, a sweet, heavy soughing passes through the trees, bending them. It's evening.

I lie here another hour or two, the birds have long since settled down, darkness is falling gently and deeply. . . . As I walk home, my feet feel their way, and I hold my hands out in front of me till I get into the open, where it is a little lighter. I walk through the hay that is still out, it's sticky and black, I slip on it because it is rotten already. When I get to the buildings I meet a bat, they fly so soundlessly, as though on wings of foam; a light chill goes through me every time they pass.

Then I stop all of a sudden.

A man appears. I can see him outlined against the new building. He is wearing a cloak, it looks like the actor's raincoat, but it's not the little actor himself. There he goes in — what next? — straight in. It's Solem.

That's where *she* is, I think, sure. Well. Alone in that big building, the South Building, Miss Torsen, sure. Solem simply went in.

I stay where I am, ready to be at hand, to run to the rescue — I'm a human being, not a brute. Some time goes by. He isn't even particularly quiet, I can hear him turning the key in there. But *now* I should hear a cry, shouldn't I? I hear nothing, nothing: a chair scrapes on the floor a bit, but no to-do. Oh well.

Good heavens, that Solem fellow may be up to

something. He may be intent upon something all right, do her some harm — he could shower her with rape! Shouldn't I knock on the window? Me — why? But at the first scream I'll be there, honestly.

No scream.

Hours go by, I've sat down, keeping watch. Obviously I can't go away and leave a helpless woman in the lurch; but hours and hours go by. A thorough business that, no trifling in there, for sure; it's now near daybreak. It occurs to me that he may be killing her, that perhaps he has killed her already; growing anxious, I am about to get up — then the key turns again in there and Solem comes out. He doesn't take to his heels, but walks back the way he came, down to my own porch, hangs the actor's raincoat where it was before and comes out again. But now he's naked. He had been in the buff in there, under the cloak. Was it possible? Oh well, nothing in the way, no delays, not a stitch. Solem had thought it all out. There he walks stark naked the few steps down to his own room.

Quite a guy, that Solem!

I sit and think, collecting myself and trying to regain my strength. What had just happened? It is still quiet in the South Building, but she can't be dead; that much I figure out by the fact that Solem walked fearlessly back to his room, turned on the light and lay down.

It relieves me to think she is alive, it cheers me up and makes me excessively brave: if he has dared to kill her, I think to myself, I'll turn him in. Then I won't spare him. I'll turn him in both for her death and the lawyer's. In fact, I'll do more, I'll turn in others, I'll turn in that thief from last winter, the one who stole flitches of bacon from some shopkeeper and sold me tobacco out of his bag. For then I won't keep mum about anything, oh no. . . .

XXIV

In the morning Solem came to the kitchen, got breakfast, was paid up by Paul and the women jointly and went back to his room. He was in no hurry; it was no longer early in the day, but he tied up his gear with great care before he went. He let his eyes rest on the windows of the South Building as he walked by.

Then Solem was gone.

A little later Miss Torsen comes in to breakfast. She asks straight off about Solem. Now, why should she be so interested in Solem, I wonder. She seemed to have lingered in her room on purpose to give him time to leave, she could've been here long ago if she

138

wanted to see him. But shouldn't she play safe and appear a bit worked up when she came in? Night owl that I am, I could after all have seen something during the night.

"Where's Solem?" she asked indignantly.

"Solem's gone," Josephine replied.

"Well, how lucky for him!"

"Why?" Josephine asked.

Oh, he was a dreadful fellow!

She was so stirred up! But she calmed down later in the day; her rage wore off, there were no tears or scenes, she just didn't walk with head held high anymore but preferred to sit still.

But that too passed; she recovered promptly and pluckily after Solem's departure, and in a couple of days she was her old self again. She took walks, chatted and laughed with us, and got the actor to push her in the swing, as the lawyer had done in his time. . . .

One evening I went for a walk, the nice weather and the darkness were just right for it, no moon, no stars. The little stream, Reisa, burbled in the hill yonder, that was all I could hear; there was God and Goethe and peace over all the peaks tonight. When I came in again I walked on tiptoe, to suit the mood I was in, and undressed and lay down in the dark.

Then they once more come back to my window,

those lunatics, Miss Torsen and her actor. What now? He certainly didn't choose this place, she chose it, figuring I'd come back again. There was something I just *had* to hear.

Why did I have to hear that he was still begging her?

"I want to make an end of it," he said, "tomorrow I'm leaving."

"I see," she replied. . . . "Oh, let's not tonight," she suddenly said, "please, some other time. All right? A little later, okay? We can talk about it tomorrow. Good night."

Then it hits me for the first time: she wants to excite you, an aging man — me, lying here — so you'll act just as crazy as the rest! That's what she wants! And now I remember back to the time before the lawyer, to Mr. Batt's first days here. I remember that she would have a kind word for me or give me a look that was out of place, as plain as her pride would allow. No, she had nothing against seeing even old age squirm. And listen to this: before, she had been anxious to appear proper and sexless, but now that was over; wasn't she right now making just a token resistance, holding out a prospect for the future? Not tonight, but a little later! she said. To be sure, a gentle refusal, a brief postponement, and I was supposed to hear it. She was so lost, but she was as wily as a madwoman. But she was so lost.

Dear child, Pharaoh laughs in front of his pyramid, he stands and laughs. He would laugh at me too.

*

The next day we three boarders are sitting in the common room. Miss Torsen and the actor are reading a book, I'm reading another.

"Would you," she asks him, "would you do me a big favor?"

"Gladly!"

"Go over to the field where we were sitting today and fetch my galoshes."

And so he went to do her a big favor. He sang a show tune as he crossed the yard, making merry in his own way.

She turned to me. "You're so quiet!"

"Am I?"

"Yes, you're so quiet."

"Listen to this," I say, starting to read from my book. I read a good-sized piece.

She tried to interrupt me several times, and finally she said impatiently, "Well, what was it I should listen to?"

"*The Three Musketeers*. You can't deny it's funny."

"I've read it before," she said. She began once more to fold her hands and pull them apart again.

"Then I'll let you hear something you haven't read before," I said, and I went to my room to get some pages I'd written. It was only some poems, nothing grand, just some short verses, little lyrics. Not that I am in the habit of reading such things aloud, but on the spur of the moment I had recourse to this to prevent her from talking more to me and demeaning herself.

While I was reading the poems to her, the actor came back.

"The galoshes weren't there," he said.

"No?" she replied absently.

"I really looked everywhere, but no."

She got up and left.

He followed her with his eyes, a bit surprised, and sat in silence for a few minutes. Then something dawned on him: "I think the galoshes must be in her hallway," he said, and hurried after her.

I went on sitting there, thinking things over. There was a sweetness in her when she said, "Yes, you're so quiet." Did she see through me and my reading? Of course. She wasn't dumb. It was probably me and no one else who was dumb, I would drive a sportsman out of his mind. Some make a sport of conquests, turning sex into a game, they think it's such fun; I've never gone in for any kind of sports. I've loved and fooled around and suffered and stormed according to my nature, nothing more. I'm old-fashioned. So here I sit in the shade of evening, in the night of the fifty-year-old. Done with that!

Then the actor came back to the common room again, discouraged and confused: she had chased him away, she was crying.

I wasn't surprised, it was a manifestation of her type.

"Can you believe it! She told me to get lost! I'm leaving tomorrow."

"Did you find the galoshes?" I asked.

"Of course!" he said. "They were standing in her own hallway. 'There they are,' I told her. 'Oh,' she said. 'They're right in front of your nose,' I said. 'Oh, get lost!' she said, and started crying. So I left."

"It'll pass."

"Yes, don't you think? It's bound to, right? Well, no one understands women, that's what I think. But they're an awesome sex, the women, a hell of an awesome sex. They really are."

He was very restless, but sat a little while before going out again.

*

That evening Miss Torsen was in the dining room before the rest of us; she was sitting there when we came in, and we all made little nods to one another. She was friendly to the actor and made up for her outburst in the afternoon.

Sitting there at the table, he finds a slip of paper in his napkin, a written note actually folded into his napkin. He's very surprised and drops what he has in his hands to unfold the note and read it. An exclamation and a smile, and his happy blue eyes leap to Miss Torsen; but since she's looking down, frowning, he sticks the note in his vest pocket.

Then it must dawn on him that he has given her away, and he has to make amends, do something. "Well, let's eat!" he says, pretending to fall to mightily.

Why did she write? She could have talked to him. He was sitting on the stairs to the porch when she came from her room and walked by. Had she counted on the good actor not being able to hold back, thus making a third party privy to their secret?

But why probe and ask any more questions! The actor didn't manage to eat much, but he looked happy all the same. So there must have been a "yes" in the note, a promise; she wouldn't chase him away anymore.

XXV

A couple of days later they are set to leave. They are leaving together — that was the upshot.

I felt like being sorry for them both; life is good but life is hard. Anyway, she must have achieved something: she'd not written him in vain, and he'd not come in vain.

So this act was over. But there are more acts, many more acts.

She had experienced a fall: once she had been robbed, she gave herself away, why save now? This is the destiny of her type: it gives itself away more and more and saves less and less; why save now? It may end in extremes: if you are halfway, why not go all the way! The type is well known, it's found at health resorts, in pensions, it flourishes and blossoms in those places.

There the woman comes with her worn-out youth, her degree and her "independence"; she comes more or less exhausted from her office stool or her schoolmistress' desk and finds herself suddenly dropped into a sweet and endless idleness, with an unlimited supply of canned goods at mealtimes. The company around her changes continually, tourists come and go, she gives herself into one hand after another for walks and conversation, the tone is "as in the country." This life is sheer frivolity, stripped of all rational purpose. She doesn't even get enough sleep; the thin wall lets through every sound from her neighbor in the adjoining room, and Anglo-Saxons coming and going slam the doors all night long. In a short while she's abnormal, fed up with people, bored with herself and with the place; if only a respectable organ grinder turned up, she would make off with him! And so she pairs off with casual strangers, such as the local tourist guide, hovering about him and twiddling rags around his fingers; eventually she goes off with some nobody who just wandered into the yard.

This is the Torsen type.

And now, at this moment, she paces about her room gathering up the pieces of herself and getting ready to leave the place — the summer is over. Ah, it takes time, there are so many pieces, one in every corner. But meanwhile she may take comfort from knowing the genitive case of *mensa*.

There's less need to worry about the actor, he hasn't lost anything, he's so frivolous; nothing goes to waste *for* him and nothing goes to waste *through* him. He leaves as he came, happy, empty and good-natured. Actually, he's more of a real man now, inasmuch as he has made a conquest. Whether he will have only happy moments with the Torsen type is another matter.

Right now he's strolling about the farm, waiting for her to get ready. When she appeared in the doorway for a moment, he called out to her, "Aren't you coming soon? We have to get over the mountain, you know."

"I can't go bareheaded, can I!" she retorted.

"No, you have to put on your hat, and that takes time! Pah!"

She gave him the once-over with a sideways look and said, "You're so — familiar."

If he then had paid her back in the same coin, there would've been tears and resentment and "Go on, go by yourself" and an hour's delay and making-up and embraces. But the actor changed his tune and, true to his nature, answered complaisantly, "Familiar? Well, maybe so. Sorry!"

Then he strolled about the farm again, singing little snatches from time to time and brandishing his stick. I notice the oddly feminine shape of his knees and his unusually heavy thighs; there was something unnatural about that heaviness, as if it didn't belong to his sex. He also wore the heels of his shoes down on the inside. And then, well, there was his V-neck and that flowing raincoat of his, which was regally draped around his shoulders even when it wasn't raining. The whole splendid apparition was ridiculous. But why speak ill of a raincoat? After all, it wasn't him, the owner, who had misused it, no, no; draped around his shoulders it was as innocent as the coat of Christ.

Why speak ill of anybody! Life is so good, but life is so hard. The moment she comes out, I think to myself, something like this may happen: I just stand there waiting for them to leave. Then she gives me her hand and says goodbye. Why don't you say something? she asks, trying to be lighthearted and jaunty. So that I won't encourage you in your great error, I reply. Ha-ha-ha, she laughs all too loudly in a strained voice, thanks! And she gets angrier and angrier, while I'm sedate and fatherly, taking my stand on the one and only right thing. I add the following memorable warning: Stop throwing yourself away, miss! Then she raises her head, yes, the Torsen type raises her head and answers, pale and offended, Throwing myself away? — I don't understand. But now it could happen, of course, that Miss Torsen, this fundamentally able and proud young woman, had a lucid moment and felt stricken: Why not, why shouldn't I throw myself away, what is there left to save? I'm already thrown away, I've been thrown away ever since my schooldays, and now I'm twenty-seven. . . .

My thoughts run away with me where I stand, and

I wish I were somewhere else. Maybe she too, pacing about her room right now, wishes I were somewhere else.

"Goodbye," I say to the actor. "Please give my regards to Miss Torsen. I have to go."

"Goodbye," he says, looking a bit surprised as he shakes my hand. "Can't you wait a little? Sure, I'll remember you to Miss Torsen. Goodbye, goodbye."

I take a short cut to seek cover, but since I know every nook and cranny I soon make a detour above the farm and find myself a good spot. From here I will be able to see them when they leave. She still had to say goodbye on the farm.

It crosses my mind that I haven't talked to her since yesterday, that we exchanged only pleasantries which I can't remember, and today I haven't spoken to her at all. . . .

There they come.

Strange — how already there seemed to be something uniting them; they walked single file up the mountain path, but they belonged to one another. They didn't talk, the most essential words had probably been said already; life had become ordinary for them, what remained was to become useful to each other. He led the way, she followed several steps behind; they looked so alone against the stony mountainside. What had become of her tall figure?

149

She appeared shorter somehow, having tied up her skirt and carrying a backpack. They each had a pack, but she carried his and he hers; she had probably brought a little more clothes and had a heavier pack. So they had exchanged loads — what sort of exchanges would they make later? After all, she was no longer a teacher, and he might not be with a theater or cinema any longer.

There they go, the two of them, climbing the stony mountain terrain, naked, with not a tree, only a few juniper bushes; far off in the hills the little stream, Reisa, is murmuring. The two of them had joined forces, and now they walked and walked; at the next stop they would be man and wife and take only one room to save money.

Suddenly I get up and feel like — out of human sympathy, you know, well, out of duty, I feel like running after her to say — come up with something, some casual word, like, Don't go any further! It could be done in a minute or two, a good deed, a duty. . . .

There they disappear behind the rocks.

Her name was Ingeborg.

XXVI

And now I too must break up again, I'm the last guest at the Tore Peak resort; it's getting late in the year, this morning it snowed for the first time — wet, sad snow.

The farm is very quiet now, and Josephine could've played the piano again and been nice to the last guest; but now I shall be leaving too. Anyway, Josephine has no reason to play and be merry, things haven't exactly gone well this year, and next year it may be worse. So, the prospects are anything but good. "But I guess we'll manage," says Josephine. There's no need to worry about her, for Josephine has money in the bank, and I'll bet she has a sweetheart on the other side of the mountain.

Oh yes, Josephine will always manage, she has such mettle. As now when Miss Torsen and her friend were leaving. The friend couldn't pay his bill, he said he had been expecting some money but it hadn't come, and now he couldn't wait any longer on account of his business. Well, when would the bill be paid, then? As soon as he got back to town, naturally, the money was there!

"But we can't be sure we'll get the money — not from him anyway," Josephine said. "We've had mum-

151

mers like him here before. And then he got under my skin the way he walked about in the yard, like it was nothing, tossing his stick in the air and catching it again. So when Miss Torsen came in to say goodbye I told her about it, and couldn't she perhaps cover his bill? Miss Torsen was appalled and asked, 'Hasn't he paid himself?' 'No,' I said, 'he has not, and this year, you know, we need every penny,' I said, 'it's been so slow compared to other years.' Well, then Miss Torsen said we would get our money, how much was it? I told her, and then she said she couldn't cover it now, but she would see to it that the money was sent, we could count on it. And I think we can, we'll get the money, if not from him. Miss Torsen will send it all right. . . ."

Then Josephine goes to fix a snack for me to take along.

Paul is also on his legs at the moment; he's not always so steady on them, but he stays on his feet anyhow. However, he has no zest for life and just shuffles about feeding the horses and chopping wood, that's all he does with himself. To be sure, there was some manure in the summer cowshed that ought to be gotten out this fall, but Paul puts it off and puts it off, so it probably won't get done. What will be will be. But this morning some wet snow fell, the first of the season, blanketing the neglected fields and the hay that was left out. So the manure will stay where it is till next spring. Poor Paul! He's basically an easy-going man, but he trudges on and on in a whirlwind; sometimes he simply smiles, knowing it's useless to trudge on — a wry smile.

His father, the old man over in the cottage, stands on his doorstep as before from time to time, lost in thought. He's probably trying to remember, for he has ninety years behind him. He feels a bit confused about the buildings on the farm, their roofs are surely too big, they might come down and get him. He asked Josephine if his hands and fingers should be allowed to run away from him over the fields every day. Then he got mittens for his hands, but he had a way of chewing on them; altogether he would eat anything he got and never experienced any pain. So they just had to be glad he was healthy and not bedridden, Josephine said.

I didn't go over the mountain like all the others; I went back the way I'd come in the spring, in the direction of the forest and the sea. It befits me to go backward, backward, never forward anymore.

I passed the hut where Solem and I had stayed together, and then came to the Lapps, those runts, the two old ones and Olga, half human and half dwarf birch. There were knives and forks stuck in the turf wall, and a kerosene lamp hung from the ceiling in this stone-age home. Olga was on the whole very good to me, but she was small and pitiful as a hen; it made me sick just to see her scurrying about sidelong to find a couple of reindeer cheeses for me.

Then I came to my own hut from last winter, where I had stayed alone for many months. I didn't go in.

Well, yes, I did go in, I had to spend the night there; but I skip that, and so I say, to be brief, that I didn't go in. Earlier today I already wrote something funny about Madame, the mouse I left behind here last spring, but I cross it out again this evening, because I'm not in the same mood anymore and there's no point to it. You might have found it amusing, my little friend, but you aren't supposed to be amused now; you must feel downcast and listen to me, there won't be much more to listen to.

Am I moralizing? I'm explaining. I'm not moralizing, I'm explaining. But if it's moralizing for me to see what's right and to say it, then I'll moralize. Can I avoid it? I see intuitively into the future, you do not — this cannot be learned from little schoolbooks, it *cannot* be learned. Don't hate me on account of that, I'll make merry later, when my strings are tuned for it. I have no control over that. But now they are tuned to a chorale. . . .

*

I leave the hut in moonlight as the day is breaking and push on in order to reach the village in good time. But I must have started out too early and pushed on too hard, for at this rate I'll reach the village by noon. What's the rush? Maybe I am in such a hurry because I sense I'm near the sea. And when I halt on the last high hill and hear the roar and catch sight of the sea beneath me, a sweetness goes through me, a greeting from another world. *Thalatta!* I say. As I busy myself with wiping my glasses, my whole body trembles; the roar from below is sleepless and wild, the song of the wilderness heightened to passion, a kind of litany. As in a dream, I descend the hill and come to the first house.

There is no one to be seen on the farm, and some childish faces quickly disappear from the windows. The place was so small and poor, but the house was of wood, only the cowshed was turf; all in all a fisherman's home. When I went in I saw it was just as poor inside as out, but the floor was clean and strewn with evergreens. There were many children; their mother was cooking something on the stove.

They offered me a chair, and I sat down and chatted a bit with a little boy or two. Since I wasn't in too much of a hurry and had no errand, the woman asked, "Well, I suppose you'll be wanting a boat?"

"A boat?" I ask in turn. For I hadn't come by sea on my way up, I'd come many miles over hill and dale from the outermost ocean. "Well, perhaps," I say, "but where would I get to then?"

"I thought you wanted a boat to the trading center," she answers, "for that's where the steamer puts in. We've rowed over so many this summer."

Great changes since the last time — the motor coaches in Stordalen seem to have altered the entire traffic situation since my days around here ten months ago.

"Where can I stay for a day or two?" I ask.

"At the trading center, out past the islets, as you can see. Well, there's also Eilert and Olaus, they're over on this side and they'll put you up, they have big houses."

She points to the two places this side of the water and I go there; it's nearly at the shore.

XXVII

A big enough house, with a spanking new, wainscoted upper story, and a new sign: LODGING FOR TRAVELERS. Here, too, the cowshed was a turf hut.

I have no idea which is Eilert and which Olaus, and as I'm trying to figure out which path to take, a man rushes up to me. Well, it's a small world, we stumble over one another, friend and foe — I recognize an acquaintance, the thief from last winter, the bacon thief. Heh-heh, what luck, what a pleasure!

That was Eilert. He had a lodging house for travelers now.

At first, it's true, he pretended he didn't recognize me, but he couldn't get away with that for very long and had to give up. And he was man enough to pull it off. "Sure, now I see!" he said. "Oh, isn't that funny! Sure, you're welcome under my roof, such as it is."

I did less well than he, it took me a while to collect my wits. When I asked him a few questions he explained it all: how the motor coaches up and down Stordalen had brought so many travelers here, and some of them wished to put up at his place before being taken by rowboat to the steamer. For as it happened, they would always come driving down in the evening, and the weather might be good or it might be bad, and the fjord was no joke many a time at night. And since people were talking, he had to find a way to give shelter to the folks who came, they couldn't sleep outdoors.

"Ah, you've turned hotelier," I say.

"You're making fun of me," he answers back, "but you shouldn't bother! I just take care of the people who come, that's all the hotel there is to it. And Olaus, my neighbor, he can't do anything else either, no matter how big he builds. Just look, there he's slapping together another house, an outhouse, I'd call it, and he keeps at it with three grown men, to get it ready for next summer. But as far as that goes, he won't have much more space than I have, and I'm not so sure that fine folks, the smart set, will put up with going way around the bend to Olaus when I have my house right here where the motor coaches stop. And besides, I was the one who started it, and if I were in Olaus's shoes I wouldn't want to just ape me, like some monkey, and start putting up folks, which he can't do right anyway. But he didn't act any better than he was, and so he lined the walls of his barn with some old sails and rugs and cardboard and went and got people to sleep there. Now me, I'd never ask smart folks and travelers to sleep in a barn, a place where you keep feed and hay for dumb cattle, if I may be that bold. But, you know, when a person has got no sense of shame and has never been in good company, then —"

"It was a good thing you came," I said, "keeping me from going to someone like that."

We walked down, with him talking and explaining the whole time. Olaus had been a bad lot again and again, to ape him the way he did.

Still, if I had known what awaited me, I would have passed by Eilert's house. But I knew nothing, I was innocent, though it didn't look that way. It can't be helped.

"If only my best room wasn't already occupied!" Eilert said. "But some fine folks from town are staying there. They came walking down through Stordalen, for the motor coaches have stopped running for this year; they've been here several days now and are likely to stay awhile yet, they were so tired out from walking. But it's a pity you can't have my best room upstairs!"

Looking up, I was met by a face in the window, a stab of emotion went through me — well, not emotion of course, far from it, but at any rate it was another surprise. What a strange coincidence, the idea of it! And as we are about to go in, there stands the actor too, looking at me, the actor from the Tore Peak

159

inn! The knees, the cloak, the stick. I thought I recognized her face in the window, all right. It's a small world.

We say hello and start to chat. Real nice to see me again! And good old Paul at Tore Peak, poor devil, was probably hitting the bottle as usual? "Gosh, what odd forms it can take: he thought the whole farm was an aquarium and that we, the guests, were goldfish! Ha-ha-ha, goldfish, no such luck, I say!" — "Oh, Eilert, you won't forget the fresh haddock for this evening, will you? Good." Ah, it was really nice here, they had already been here for several days and were staying awhile longer to rest up.

As we stand there a fat maid comes down from upstairs and speaks to the actor, "The missus wants you to come up right away."

"Oh? All right, this minute. . . . Well, so long, see you later. So you'll be staying here?"

He hurried upstairs.

Eilert and I followed him up to my room.

*

However, I went back out with Eilert right away, he had so much to explain and instruct me about, and I didn't mind listening to him now. Eilert wasn't at all bad, he was a splendid roughneck in any case, with four fine ragged children by his first wife, who had died two years ago, and another one by his new wife. When he told me this he must have forgotten the cock-and-bull story he related to me last winter, about a sick wife and ailing children. The maid who came down from upstairs with the message from missus wasn't a maid at all but Eilert's young wife. And she was not so bad, strong and buxom, good with the animals, and pregnant again.

I think it's all great — Eilert, his wife, and everything I'm hearing about them.

However, nobody will understand what I had to be so strangely pleased about right then, but a vague happiness started up in me when I came to this house a while ago. It was probably just coincidence, but even so it was just as nice a feeling to me; I was happy about everything and found it all very jolly. There were those ewes by the shed, they were so cuddly — the children had slept with them and kissed them and ridden on them ever since they were small; and of course there was that one goat on the roof, standing so close to the edge it was a wonder it didn't get dizzy. Gulls were flying here and there over the fields, uttering their own sounds to each other and being friends and enemies as best they could; and right at the mouth of the river, directly below where the sun used to set, began the long road that ran through the woods and up the valley. The end of such a road coming down from the forest can have all the friendliness of a living being.

Then Eilert was going haddock-fishing, and I went along. He didn't really have the time for it, he should've been getting some meat for us, but he'd given his promise to the gentry from town, and besides fish were also God's gift. If he wound up short on meat, he would just slaughter a ewe.

It's blowing some; but it should blow a bit, as long as it didn't blow too much, Eilert says. Still, he doesn't quite trust the weather tonight, he tells me, looking at the sky; freshening wind, a strong draft. At first I'm quite brave and even take note of Eilert's French words as I sit there on my thwart: *prekevere*, *travali*, *sutinere*, *mankement*, and many more; they have followed a beaten path, having come here through the ancient connection with Bergen, and now they are common property.

Then I don't bother with French words anymore, I feel so sick. Anyway, it's blowing too hard, and we aren't catching any haddock. "It was too bad she came on us so fast," Eilert says, "let's try over there, closer to the shore."

But we don't catch anything there either, and the

wind freshens and the sea swells. "We'd better be rowing home," Eilert says.

Hmm, the sea was suitably ruffled a moment ago — how strange that a little while ago it was just right; but now it was too much. Why on earth did I feel so miserable? An inner exhaustion or some agitation would have explained it, but I hadn't felt any agitation.

The sea foams at the bow, the waves crest and break around the boat. "It's terrible how fast she rises, isn't it?" Eilert says, rowing hard.

Then I feel so awful that Eilert tells me to ship my oars, he'll manage alone. But miserable as I am, I know they can see me from the shore, so I don't ship the oars. Eilert's wife might see me and laugh at me.

Ugh, what a disgusting sickness that seasickness is, forcing me to lean over the side and make a mess! Afterward I feel a moment's relief, but then it starts again, oh, how charming! It's as though I were giving birth, the wrong way, of course, up through my throat, but giving birth. It comes part way, stops at a catch, it comes and stops, comes and stops. It's an iron catch — iron, did I say? Steel. I never had it before, and I wasn't born with it. It brings my whole machinery to a halt. I take a running start from way down inside me and let out a strange howl; but a howl, however

163

successful, cannot break a steel catch. The labor pains go on. My mouth is coated with bile. Please God, won't my chest spring a leak pretty soon? "Oh . . . !"

Then we make it to the lee of the islands, and I'm saved.

All at once I'm fine again and do a few tricks, mimicking myself out there, just to fool those on shore. And I assure Eilert too that this was the first time, to make him understand it wasn't worth being bruited about. He had no idea what seas I had stood up to without suffering the least discomfort; at one time twenty-four days at sea, most everyone else done in, the captain himself retching like a woman — but me?

"You know, I'm bothered by seasickness myself sometimes," Eilert says.

I ate supper alone in the living room. Since there was no haddock on the table, the strangers upstairs refused to come down. They only wanted some bread and butter and milk brought up, Eilert's wife said.

XXVIII

In the morning they were gone.

Sure enough, about four o'clock, at daybreak — I heard clearly when they left, I was sleeping so near the stairs. There he came with his fat thighs, his feet clumping heavily; she shushed him, sounding angry.

Eilert had just gotten up himself. They stood outside for a while, dickering about getting a boat — right away, this minute! They had changed their minds and wanted to get going. I saw them walk down to the boat with Eilert in tow, and noticed they were impatient with each other in the early-morning chill. There had been frost overnight, the puddles were iced over, and the ground felt hard to walk on. Poor things, no breakfast, no coffee; a windy morning, with some choppiness left over from last night. There they go down to the boat with their packs in place, and she has her red hat on.

Well, it was none of my business and I lay down again, intending to sleep till midday or so. I had no business with anybody, only with myself. Since I couldn't see the boat from my bed I got up again for a moment, for the fun of it, to see how far they had gone. Not very far, though both men rowed. A while later I again got up to look — well, yes, they were making progress. I took my stand by the window; it was kind of fun to watch the boat getting smaller and smaller, I opened the window and used my field glasses. Since it wasn't quite light yet, I couldn't make out anything very clearly, but I could see the red hat. Then the boat disappeared behind the islets.

I dressed and went down; the children were all asleep in the living room, but the wife, Regine, was up. How calmly and naturally the good Regine took everything!

"Do you know what's become of your husband?" I ask.

"Well, have you ever seen the likes!" she answers. "I saw them only the moment they made off — down to the shore. Where were they going, I wonder — haddock-fishing?"

"Maybe," I simply say. But to myself I thought, No, they were obviously skipping out, since they had their backpacks on.

"Ever seen the likes," Regine says again, "no breakfast, no coffee, nothing! And the missus didn't get to eat anything yesterday evening either!"

I just shook my head and walked away. Regine called after me that the coffee was almost ready, so if I wanted a cup, then —.

Naturally I could only shake my head and walk away on hearing such abysmal folly. And stick with the one and only right thing. And refuse to understand or fathom men and women who behaved in that way. But I, yours truly, should probably have moved to Olaus's place yesterday instead of going angling. Then I would have done what was even more right. What business did I have here anyway? It might very well be that she who now styled herself missus had gotten in hot water, and that this was the reason she didn't get to eat yesterday evening, and didn't manage to be down today. And so she withdrew, with her friend and her pack.

Well, one may not have very much to withdraw with, that probably doesn't matter very much. As long as one has something to withdraw for.

*

Eilert was home again by mid-morning. He didn't bring the guests back with him, but he was carrying one of their packs up from the landing when he came. Their biggest pack. Angry and annoyed, he said that nobody could fool around with him, no, they couldn't.

It was the bill again, naturally.

She'll probably have to go through plenty of that sort of thing, I think to myself; but she'll soon get listless, I suppose, and take it as naturally as it should be taken. There are worse things.

But, in any case, I was the one who had disturbed them and chased them off without their togs; maybe they were really waiting for some money, what did the rest of us know?

I got hold of Eilert. How big was that bill, what

167

amount? Oh, that was nothing, nothing at all. "There you are! And now, row straight back to the trading station with those clothes!"

But this proved to no avail, the strange couple had taken the boat right away — they had made it just in time — and were already on board.

Nothing to be done.

"But here's the address," Eilert says, "we can send the clothes next Thursday when the steamer goes south again."

I took the address and told Eilert off. Why had he seized just this pack, why not the other?

He answers that the gentleman had in fact offered him the other bag, but Eilert could tell from its looks that there was nothing in it. And I ought to bear in mind that the money the missus had given him paid for only one of them. So it was only fair that he'd taken the fullest pack. All in all Eilert had behaved modestly, nobody could say anything else. For when the missus had shushed him, handed over the bigger pack and written down her address, he for his part had kept perfectly quiet and not said another word. Anyway, nobody should come and fool around with him! They had better not!

Eilert threw up a long arm, clenching his fist.

But once he'd eaten and had coffee and rested up

he was no longer so irritable and became as expansive as yesterday. He'd been thinking hard and mulling things over ever since last summer when the motor coaches started, and how would I feel if he also hired three grown men and built an even bigger house than Olaus?

Good Lord, he too had caught the disease, the modern Norwegian epidemic!

But once again, there was the bag in the couple's room. They were her clothes, all right, I recognized her blouses, skirts and shoes from the summer. I hardly looked at them, just took them out, folded them nicely and packed them away again; I suspect Eilert had rummaged through them. That was the sole reason I opened the bag.

XXIX

I was to experience yet another party of Englishmen, yes, indeed, the last ones for this year.

They had come by the steamer this morning and had been staying at the trading station since then; from there they had sent a messenger up the valley for a motor coach to pick them up. "Stordalen, Stordalen!" they had cried. So Stordalen must still have been an unknown valley to them — a blot on their name they would no longer tolerate.

And what a commotion they made!

They came by boat from the trading center, we heard them from far away, one old voice out-shouting all the others. Eilert dropped everything and ran down to the landing to be first, but from Olaus's house a man and some teenagers also went down — in fact, from every house nearby there came people ready to run and to serve. There were so many onlookers at the landing that the old man with the voice rose to his full stature in the boat and shouted his English at us — as if taking for granted that *his* language was also *ours*: "Where is the motor coach? Get us a motor coach!"

And Olaus, who was smart and guessed what it was about, at once dispatched his teenagers up the valley to have a motor coach sent express. The English were here!

They stepped ashore and were in a great hurry, unable to understand why the motor coach wasn't there. What was the idea? There were four of them; "Stordalen!" they said. As they walked up to Eilert's house they looked at their watches and swore at the minutes they were losing. "Where the hell is the motor coach?" And everyone tagged along and stared in awe at the dressed-up idiots.

I remember a couple of them: an old man, the one with the voice, who was wearing plus fours — a skirt on each thigh! — and a green canvas jacket with lacings and straps and buckles and a myriad pockets. Oh, what a man, what vigor! His beard was white and green, it fluttered down from his nose like the northern lights, and he swore like crazy. Another one of the company was tall and stooped, a young beanpole, unbelievable, with sloping shoulders and a tiny little cap sitting on his loftily arched eyebrows; he looked like an upraised Roman battering ram, he was a man on stilts. Trying to size him up, I'm left with plenty that my eyes cannot cover. But he was stooped and broken-down, old before his time, completely bald; and yet, believe it or not, his mouth was grimly set, like a tiger's, and he had a craze in his head that kept him on his legs! "Stordalen!" he said.

England will soon have to establish old folks' homes for its children, most likely. It unsexes its people with sport and fixed ideas; if Germany hadn't kept it in a state of perpetual uneasiness, it would have turned to pederasty in a couple of generations. . . .

Then the motor coach hoots up in the woods, and they all set off in a mad rush, racing to meet it.

But now that Olaus's two teenagers had been way up the road to find the motor coach and hurry it on,

171

and all in good faith, shouldn't they get something for it? True enough, they'd been taken along and had enjoyed the ride of a lifetime, but what about pay? They have picked up enough nerve this summer not to give in, they go to the old man with the voice and hold out their hands: "Our pay!" But the old man balks and simply climbs in, hurrying up the others. And the driver, with his mind on his own tips, probably thinks he will serve the travelers most devotedly by driving off at once. So off they go! A toot on the horn, a roaring shindy, tararaboomdeay!

Then the onlookers go home, all the while talking about those grand visitors. From abroad, yes, from abroad — oh no, our own countrymen had better stand back! Did you see the height of that one lord? And did you see the other one, the guy with the britches and the northern lights?

But some of the returning gawkers, the Olaus family, had more serious things on their minds. The father now understood for the first time what he'd read so often in the papers: that the schools for Norway's children were still miserably poor, since they didn't learn English. His boys had doubtless missed out on a nice piece of cash just because they couldn't curse back at Northern Lights intelligibly. And the boys themselves had plenty to think about as well: the driver, that crook, that southerner! But just you wait! They had heard that broken glass, half hidden in the road, was so good for rubber tires. . . .

*

I go upstairs again to the bag with her clothes, and the reason I do so is that Eilert is not to be trusted. I want to count the garments so that none disappear, it was a mistake not to do it first thing in the morning.

It might look as if I came back to these clothes again and again and kept thinking about them; but why should I? It now appeared, however, I had been right to be suspicious of Eilert; I'd heard him go upstairs, and when I came up he was standing over the clothes, spreading them out. "*What?*" I said. He tried at first to act uppity toward me: I'd better not fool with him! But I knew something about him, and that gave me an overwhelming edge; he thought it over, and soon he stopped champing at the bit. But how I wronged him, bleeding him white!

"You didn't buy these clothes," he said. "I might have gotten a lot more for them."

His bill had been paid but he wanted more, he was like a stomach that continues digesting after death. That was Eilert. Still, he wasn't all that bad, he'd never been any better nor gotten any worse in his new business.

If only none would be any worse in their new business!

I took the bag with the clothes into my own room, to better watch them. It was a big chore to fold them nicely again a second time, but it had to be done. Later in the evening I would go my way and take the bag with me; I was done with the place, and there was a moon at night now.

Oh, enough about those clothes.

XXX

One has reached an age, you see, when one walks by moonlight again. Thirty years ago one also walked by moonlight, walked over snow-covered roads that crunched underfoot, over black frost in the field, around unlocked hay barns, hunting for love. Oh, yes. Do I remember! But there is no such moonlight any-more — good God, I could read the letter she had sneaked to me by it. And there are no such letters anymore.

Everything has changed, the adventure is over, to-night I am on an errand merely of the head: I'm go-ing to the trading center to send a bag by the steamer, and then I'll go on, walking and walking. Yes, and for that I need just an ordinary hiker's smarts and a little moonlight to see by. But in the old days, in my youthful days, we were studying the almanac already in the fall to see if there would be moonlight on Twelfth Night. We needed it so badly.

Everything has changed, I have changed. The adventure is in the adventurer.

They say that age brings joys one hasn't had before, deeper and more lasting joys. It's a lie. Yes, you read correctly: it's a lie. It's the aged themselves who say that, the selfish person waving the banner of his remains. He no longer remembers the time when he stood on the summit, his own alias, crimson and white, blowing a golden trumpet. Now he doesn't stand — oh no, he has sat down, it's easier to sit. And now there comes to him, with halting steps, fat and stupid, the honor of old age. What use is honor to a sitting man? A standing man can use it, a sitting man can only have it. But honor is to be used, not to sit down with.

Give a sitting man warm socks.

*

What a coincidence: imagine coming across an unlocked hay barn, just as in my golden-trumpet days!

It invites me with piles of hay and with shelter for the night; but where is the girl who gave me the letter? I remember, don't I, how sweet her breath was — and didn't I feel her lips parting? She'll come back, just wait, time is on our side, another twenty years, she's sure to come back. . . .

I have to be on my guard not to mistake this for something other than the malice that it is. For I've reached the age of honor, I'm debilitated, I'm capable of seeing a good barn as a courtesy from above: thou most deserving age, here is a hay barn for you!

But no thanks, I'm only in my early seventies.

So I pass by the barn, obeying my head's errand.

Toward morning I find shelter under a cliff. It will suit me to live under cliffs hereafter; there I lie hugging myself, curled up and small and invisible. Anything, anything, rather than waving the selfish banner of what remains!

I'm fine now, putting the stranger's pack of used clothes under my head only because it's about the right size. But sleep won't come, only thoughts and dreams and lines of verse and sentimentality. Since the pack smells of people, I toss it away and lie on my arm. My arm smells of wood, not even wood.

But the scrap with the address — I still have the address, don't I? Good. I light a match and peruse it, so I'll know it for tomorrow. Just a few words in pencil, nothing; but there was a softness about the letters maybe, something feminine, I don't know. Never mind.

I see to it that I reach the trading center not too early in the day, everyone is up and about, the post office is open. I get a big piece of paper and string and sealing wax, wrap and seal the whole thing and write the address on the outside. There you are!

O-o-h — I forgot the slip with the address, to put it inside, I mean; well, I never! But otherwise it's all done. As I go my way I feel strangely empty and forlorn; that pack was pretty heavy after all, and now I'm rid of it. The last joy! — the word pops into my head. Apropos of nothing in particular, I think to myself, The last country, the last island, the last joy. . . .

XXXI

What now?

At first I didn't know. Winter lay ahead, my summer was behind me, no tasks, no aspirations, no ambitions. Since it didn't matter where I stayed, I happened to think of a city I knew, I could go there — why not? A man cannot sit by the sea forever, and if he decides to leave it behind him, that doesn't have to be misconstrued. And so he interrupts his solitude, as others have done before him, feeling a bit curious to see all the ships and all the horses and the little frozen gardens in a certain city. And once there, he may in his idleness begin to wonder if he shouldn't know someone in this city, this terribly big city. There's a nice moon now, and it amuses him to give himself a certain address to go by night after night, and to post himself there as though it were a matter of some importance. He's not expected anywhere else, so he has the time for it. And one night someone finds him reading under a street lamp; she stops at once and stands there a moment, then takes a few steps toward him, leaning forward, scrutinizing him. "Aren't you —? No, excuse me, I thought —"

"Right. Good evening, Miss Torsen."

"Oh, good evening. I thought it was you, all right. Good evening. — Very well, thank you. And thank you for the bag; I knew at once, I know very well that —"

"Do you live here? What an odd coincidence."

"Yes, I live here, those are my windows. I don't suppose you'd come up? — Oh, I see."

"But I know of some benches down here on the dock," I say. "If you won't be cold?"

"No, I'm not cold. Thanks, I'd like to."

We went down to the benches, like a father and

daughter out walking. There was nothing conspicuous about us in any way and we were undisturbed all
evening. Later we were also left undisturbed other
evenings, short, friendly evenings all through a cold
fall month.

She told me first the short chapter of her trip home,
some things only hinted at, others related more fully,
at times hiding her face, at times — when I asked
questions — giving brief answers or shaking her head.
I write it down from memory; it became important
for her, it became important for others.

Anyway — in a hundred years it will all be forgotten. Why do we struggle? In a hundred years someone will read about it in memoirs and letters and think,
How she struggled, how she toiled, heh-heh! There
are others about whom nothing will be written or
read, life has shut them up in a grave. It's all one. . . .

The sort of worries she had, oh, what worries! At
the time when she didn't have enough money to pay
her lodging house bill she was at the center of the
world, everything was staring at her and her head was
buzzing with bewilderment. Then she heard a man
in the yard asking, "Hasn't Sorrel been watered yet
today?" That was *his* worry. So she was not at the
center of the world, after all.

Then she and her friend left the inn, they were on

their way. Center of the world? Not a bit of it. Day after day over the mountain, day after day down through the valley, eating whenever they happened on a house, drinking from the streams. When they met other wayfarers they exchanged greetings or they did not, nobody was less at the center of the world than they were, and nobody more. Her friend, empty and happy-go-lucky, whistled as he went along.

At one stop they had a bite to eat.

"Pay for me for now, will you," he said.

She hesitated and then simply answered that she couldn't pay for him the whole way.

"No, of course not, far from it," he said. "Only for the time being; further down the valley we can get a loan maybe."

"I don't borrow."

"Ingeborg!" he said, whimpering playfully.

"What is it?"

"Nothing. I can call my wife Ingeborg, can't I?"

"I'm not your wife, not a bit," she replied, getting up.

"Whoa! We certainly were man and wife last night. It says so in the guest book."

She let that pass. All right, they were man and wife last night to save a room, to travel sensibly. But she'd been very stupid to agree to it.

"But Miss Torsen!" he said, whining.

To put an end to this playacting she paid for them both and picked up her pack.

On they went. At the next stop she paid for them both without a word — for supper, for the bed, and for breakfast. It began to be a habit. On they went again. When they reached the end of the valley and found themselves by the sea, she rebelled again: "You just go — go away! I don't want you in my room anymore!"

The old arguments didn't work this time. When he repeated that it saved them money, she replied she needed only one room for herself, and that she could pay for. Speaking playfully again, he whined, "Ingeborg!" and walked off. He was helpless, his back drooped.

She ate supper alone.

"Isn't your husband coming?" the mistress asked.

"He probably doesn't want anything," she answered.

He stood over by the little cow barn, pretending he was interested in the roof, in the way it was built; he walked about looking at things, pursing his lips and whistling. But she could plainly see through the window that his face looked sad and blue. When she had finished eating she walked down to the sea, calling to him on the way, "Go in and eat!"

But that spineless he was not; he didn't go in to eat and he didn't have a roof over his head that night.

But the outcome was the usual one: when she finally found him the next morning and repented, shaken by his appearance, everything drifted back to normal again.

During the couple of days they stayed there waiting for the packet boat, an elderly man came to the house one evening. She knew him and he knew the couple; she was terribly upset and got ready to leave at once, crying and beating her breast — she wanted to go home, away, at once. The outcome was as usual: when she got hold of herself she settled down for the night. She was not the center of the world, nor did the old acquaintance who had arrived appear to stare only at her. Yet, early the next morning, in the gray light of dawn before anyone else was up, she got her way and effected a sort of escape. That much she did.

After boarding the packet boat she met no more acquaintances and could think things over in peace. At this point she broke in earnest with her friend. They had another small disagreement — he had no ticket, and one word led to another. It was easy for her, he said, sitting there with a return ticket in her pocket. Anyway, it was her letter last summer which had got him into all this trouble. Wasn't she ashamed? He wouldn't have taken a step out of town if it hadn't been for her letter. Then she gave him her purse, all her money, and told him to get lost. There was probably just enough for his ticket, now she was rid of him. "I shouldn't accept this of course, but it can't be helped," he said and left.

She gazed far out to sea, taking stock. Things were going very badly for her now, so differently from what she had once imagined. What a shameful mess, what crazy nonsense she'd gotten mixed up in! After ruminating till she got tired, she began to listen to what the people around her were talking about. Sitting each on his own chest, a couple of fellows were buddying up to shelter themselves from the wind; she heard one of them say he was a teacher and that the other one was a kind of craftsman. The teacher didn't sit for long, but minced up to her; she walked silently past him and took his place on the chest.

It was fall and raw weather, it felt good to be out of the wind. The craftsman probably figured that the tall, well-dressed woman had a cabin to herself, but when she came and sat down on his chest, he moved over. He was getting ready to smoke his pipe but stopped.

"Please, go ahead and smoke," she said.

Then he lit up, but turned well away and didn't blow smoke in her face.

He was very young, in his early twenties, with thick reddish hair under his cap and whitish eyebrows high on his forehead. His chest was broad and flat, but his back was round and his hands massive. Heavens, what an ox!

Someone brought him food, sandwiches and coffee, which he must have been waiting for; he paid but went on smoking and let the food sit.

"Go ahead and eat," she said. "It doesn't matter that I'm sitting here, does it?"

"Oh no," he answered. He knocked out his pipe, taking his time, and remained seated. "I really don't need any food yet," he said.

"You haven't been traveling long, then?"

"No, only tonight. Where are you from?"

"From town. I've been on vacation."

"I thought so," he said, nodding.

"I've been staying at the Tore Peaks," she added.

"The Tore Peaks? Really?"

"You know the place?"

"No. I just know some people there." Pause. "Josephine, she's there."

"Yes. You know her?"

"Well, no."

As the boat sailed on they chatted some more; they had nothing better to do sitting there. She asked where he was from and what sort of trade he was in, and he was nothing much, just a miserable cabinetmaker; well, his mother had a small farm. Wouldn't she like a simple cup of coffee?

Yes, thanks, she would have a drop of his, in the saucer.

She poured coffee for herself onto the saucer and asked for a bite to eat as well. Never had a mouthful of food tasted better to her, and when she was finished she thanked him accordingly.

"Well, I suppose you have a cabin?" he asked.

"Sure, but I'd rather sit here," she replied. "If I go below I get sick."

"I thought as much. Oh, I really wonder if —?" And with that he got up and lumbered slowly away. She saw his back disappear down the companionway to the lower deck.

She waited a long time for him, afraid that someone might come and take his seat. Coffee from the saucer, a good-sized sandwich with a cabinetmaker, no affectation or tricks — there really seemed to be a small foothold for her in this corner.

There he came back with more food and coffee, a whole tray in his big hands. He laughed good-naturedly at himself for walking so gingerly.

She clapped her hands together, exaggerating a little, "What on earth! Oh, you're really too kind."

"I thought, since you were sitting here anyway —"

They both ate, she felt warm and drowsy, sat back and fell half asleep. Each time she opened her eyes the cabinetmaker was lighting his pipe; he struck two or three matches at a time, but since he was in no hurry the matches were half gone before he put the pipe in his mouth and started pulling at it. The teacher shouted something to him, wanting him to notice something far inland, but the cabinetmaker only nodded and said nothing. Maybe he's afraid of waking me? she thought.

At one of the stops her traveling companion popped up again, emerging from the cabin. "Aren't you coming down, Ingeborg?" he asked.

She didn't answer.

The cabinetmaker looked at them both by turns.

"But Miss Torsen!" her companion whined again, trying to be playful. He waited a moment, then went away.

Ingeborg, the cabinetmaker probably thought to himself. Miss Torsen, he probably thought.

"How long will you be in town?" she asked, sitting up.

"I figured on staying there awhile."

"What will you be doing there?"

He became slightly embarrassed, and since he had such light skin you could tell right away when he blushed. He leaned forward and placed his elbows on his knees before answering: "I would like to learn my trade a little better, apprentice myself. But it all depends."

"I see. Uh-huh."

"What do you think about it?" he asked.

"Well, it sounds very good."

"You think so?"

They stayed on deck almost all day; in the afternoon it turned bitter cold, there was a wind blowing. When she got stiff with sitting she stood up and stamped her feet, when she got tired from standing she sat down on the chest again. At a point where she stood a little way off, the cabinetmaker put a parcel on the chest as though to save her seat for her.

Her traveling companion stuck his head through the door, the wind blowing his hair over his eyes as he shouted, "Go below, won't you, Ingeborg!"

"Ugh!" she groaned. Suddenly flying into a rage, she went at him, being carried along as the ship heeled over; she made a couple of hops and hissed, "I won't hear another word from you. Understand? As God is my witness!"

"Gee!" he said, and disappeared.

Around three o'clock the cabinetmaker brought more coffee and eatables.

"Oh, you really shouldn't give me anymore," she said.

He just laughed his good-natured laugh again, and please, she should just help herself.

"We'll soon be arriving," she said as they ate. "Do you have someone to go to?"

"Oh yes, that I do. A sister."

Slowly and gingerly, he took another sandwich, turned it around and looked at it dreamily before taking a bite. When he had finished a mouthful he took another one. When he had finished that one too, he said, "Well, I figured that if I stayed here in town all winter I couldn't help learning something. And with the farm on top of it —"

"Uh-huh."

"You think so too?"

"Oh yes. Sure I do."

Why did he tell her about his private affairs? She had her own affairs. She thanked him for the refreshments and stood up.

When the boat docked he shook her hand and said, "My name is Nikolai."

"Yeah?"

"Just in case we should happen to meet again —
Nikolai Palm — but I guess the city is too big —"

"Yes, I guess so. But thank you so much for everything. Goodbye."

XXXII

"Have you seen the cabinetmaker since?" I ask Miss
Torsen.

"What cabinetmaker? Oh, no. I only told you about
him because he was a sort of acquaintance."

"Acquaintance?"

"Both yours and mine. Well, only in a way, of
course. It turns out he's the brother of Miss Palm,
the teacher who was with us at the Tore Peaks this
summer."

"Well, it's a small world. We're all one family."

"That's why I told you all those things about him."

"But you didn't find out about this connection on
the ship," I said, "so I suppose you've seen him since?"

"Well, no — I mean I've seen him a couple of
times but not talked to him. We only said hello and
how are you doing? and such. Then he told me he
was her brother."

"Heh-heh!"

"Just in passing, you know, quite by chance."

This was a good opportunity for me to say, "What's not by chance? It was by chance that I stopped under that street lamp to look up something, to peruse a couple of lines. And then you lived there."

"Yes, that's right."

"You and the cabinetmaker may be a pair some day."

"Ha-ha. I won't be pairing off with anybody."

"No?"

"One has to be pretty naive to get married."

"I don't know, maybe it doesn't hurt to be a little naive. A little less clever. What does cleverness lead to? To falling short. You see, no one is clever enough."

"But shouldn't cleverness help us fall short as seldom as possible? What else is it good for?"

"Right, what else is it good for? But the trouble is that we rely too much on our cleverness, and so we fall short. Or we let things ride — please yourself! — we have our cleverness to fall back on."

"So it's hopeless, isn't it?"

"Well, yes, to go that way. And this was your opinion too, this summer."

"Yes, I remember. I thought — oh, I don't know. But then I got back to town again, and it was like —"

Pause.

"I'm confused," she said.

"And I'm old and wise. You see, Miss Torsen, in the old days people's heads weren't so full of cleverness and schooling and voting rights, they lived their lives in a different way, they were simple. I wonder if that isn't a stronger wall to lean on. People fell short then too, but they didn't have to pay such a high price for it; they bore up with their greater animal vigor. We have sapped our healthy tolerance for bearing up."

"It's getting cold," she said. "Shouldn't we go home? What you're saying is perfectly true, of course, but we live in the present. We can't change anything — anyway, all *I* can do is to keep up with things."

"That's what it says in *Morgenbladet*, sure, because the *Neue Freie Presse* said it first. But anybody who's good for something goes his own way to some extent, leaving right-thinking mediocrity to its fate."

"Yes. But now I have to tell you something," she said and stopped. "I'm going to a sensible school these days."

"You are?"

"But this time I'm learning housekeeping, isn't that nice?"

"You're learning how to cut your own bread?"

"Ha-ha."

"You aren't getting married, after all!"

"Oh, I don't know."

"Good. You get married, you settle down in his valley. But first you want to learn housekeeping so you can make an omelet or a pudding for some tourist or Englishman who might happen by."

"His valley? What valley?"

"You'd do better to visit his mother and learn all the housekeeping you need from her."

"Now look here!" she says, laughing and starting to walk again, "you're on the wrong track completely. It's not him, it's no one."

"Too bad for you. It should be someone."

"Yes, but what if it isn't the one I want?"

"But he *is* the one you want. A tall and attractive and capable woman like you!"

"Thanks, but still. Well, thank you for a nice evening. Good night. . . ."

Why did she break off so suddenly and rush off, almost running? Was she crying? I would have liked to say more, I could have been wise and boring and dropped helpful hints, now I just stood there in shamefaced wonder.

Then something happened.

"I haven't seen you for so long," she said the next time we met. "So nice bumping into you. Will you walk with me for a moment? I was bringing —"

"A letter, I see."

"Yes, a letter. It's just — it's nothing —"

We went to the newspaper office with the letter. It must have been a want ad, maybe she was applying for a job.

As she came out of the office a gentleman greeted her. She turned crimson. She stopped briefly near the top of the stairs, two stone steps above street level, lowering her head to her chest as though she were watching out carefully for those two steps coming down. They said hello once more, the stranger shook her hand and they started to talk.

It was a man her own age, good-looking, with a soft, blond full beard and dark eyebrows, maybe blackened. He wore a top hat, and his overcoat, which was open, had a silk lining.

I heard them talk about an evening the previous week they had both enjoyed; they'd had a little fling, a whole group of them — a drive, a late dinner, a memorable evening. Miss Torsen didn't say much, she stood lost in thought, laughing softly, handsome. I started looking at some illustrated magazines in the window, but suddenly I thought, My goodness, she's in love!

"Listen, I have a suggestion," he said. They made

some arrangement, agreed on something, she nodded. Then he left.

She comes over to me, slowly and silently. I draw her attention to one of the pictures in the window. "Yes," she says, "just imagine!" She stares, but sees nothing. We start walking in silence and say nothing for a few minutes.

"Hans Flaten is always true to form," she says.

"Now, who was that gentleman?" I ask.

"His name's Flaten."

"I seem to remember you mentioned his name this summer. What does he do?"

"His father is a merchant."

"What about himself?"

"His father has that big store on Alme Street."

"Hmm, but himself, what does he do?"

"I don't know that he does anything in particular, he's a student. His father being so rich and all."

I jogged my memory: old man Flaten's business on Alme Street was a solid country store, and every morning there were always several farm horses standing in the courtyard while the owners did their shopping inside.

"He's always so suave," she went on, "God, you should see how calmly he puts his money on the table — banknotes. Wherever he goes people whisper:

194

That's Flaten."

I tried to be witty and said, "He dresses as if his name were von Platen."

"So?" she said, offended. "Sure, he dresses fashionably, he always did."

"Is he the one you want?" I asked facetiously.

She was silent a moment, then said with a decisive nod, "Yes."

"What, him?"

"Is that so strange? We're old friends, we were classmates in high school, we've spent a lot of time together. It rests on a solid foundation. He's the only man I've ever been in love with, it's been going on for years. True, I forget him at times, but as soon as I see him again I'm as badly smitten as ever. I've told him about it and we both laugh, but that doesn't change anything. I'm so funny that way."

Then he must be too rich for her, I thought, and asked no more questions.

As we parted, however, I asked, "Where does the cabinetmaker, Nikolai, work?"

"I don't know. Yes, come to think, I do know. It's on my way, if you walk a bit further with me I'll show you. What do you want with him?"

"Nothing. I just wondered if he'd found a good place, a competent master."

*

Yes, indeed, what did I want with Nikolai, with the craftsman! And yet I've now been to see him and have gotten to know him. Built like a horse, strong and ugly, and terribly closemouthed. Saturday evening we took in the town together, I don't know why, but I was the one who suggested it.

I kept company with the cabinetmaker on my own account, on account of my loneliness, for I didn't go to sit on the benches at the dock anymore. The weather had turned cold and Miss Torsen was of little interest to me now, having backslided again since she got back to the city; she had become more ordinary and girlish not only in this or that, but in everything. She thought of nothing but vanity and nonsense and seemed to have completely forgotten the bitter but sound view of her life that she had last summer. Now she'd ended up in school again, in her spare time she used to see a gentleman named Flaten, and so she was kept busy. Either she must be lacking in depth of character, or she had become warped during the crucial years of her youth.

"What shall I do?" she said. "Certainly I've gone back to school again, that's what I've been doing since I was little. I'm no good at anything else, I'm only good at doing my lessons, that's what I'm used to. I cannot think or do much of anything on my own, nor is it any fun. So what shall I do?"

Yes, what should she do!

Nikolai the cabinetmaker got to see the circus, but there was little to marvel at, or he pretended that what they offered wasn't very remarkable. That jump on the horse — sure, but still! That tiger — I thought tigers were much bigger. Anyway, his slow, powerful head seemed to be busy with some other thought, and he didn't pay much attention when the equestriennes were doing their tricks.

On the way home he said, "I'm ashamed to ask you, but would you come with me to 'Kronen' tomorrow night?"

"'Kronen,' what's that?"

"They dance there."

"Oh, a dance hall. Where is it? Do you like to dance that badly?"

"Not really, but still."

"You just want to see what's going on there?"

"Yes."

"I'll come."

＊

It was Sunday night, a night belonging to boys and girls, and the cabinetmaker and I were on our way to the dance.

He had tricked himself out with a dress shirt and a heavy watch chain — oh, he was so young, and the young look good in anything. With his unusual physical strength, he never needed to yield, and that had made him slow and self-assured. When someone talked to him he took his time answering, if someone slapped him on the shoulder he turned around slowly to see who it was. He was gentle and good to be with.

We went to the ticket window — no one there, the window was closed. A sign announced that the premises were reserved by a private party for the first two hours of the evening.

Several young people came up while we were standing there, read the sign and left. The cabinetmaker didn't want to leave, he looked around and stepped further inside the gate, as though looking for someone.

"There's nothing we can do about it," I called after him.

"No," he said, "but I wonder —." With that he went all the way into the courtyard, peering up into all the windows.

A man comes down the stairs.

"What can I do for you?"

"I guess he wants a ticket," I replied. The cabinetmaker would never get done.

The man came over to me, he turned out to be the landlord. He told me what the sign said: a private party had leased the hall for the first two hours.

"So there's nothing we can do about it," I called to my friend.

But he took his time before coming, I chatted a little with the landlord while I waited.

"Yes, a high class party," he said. There were supposed to be only eight couples, but with a big band, so they must be rich. Sure, now and then parties of fashionable people leased the hall for a few hours, bringing refreshments and plenty of champagne. Then they danced for dear life. Why they did it? Youth, wealth, upperclass people, Sunday night boredom at home — they wanted to work off a whole week's idleness in those two hours, so they danced. It wasn't really so strange. "And I make more in that bit of time than I do all night otherwise," the landlord said. Big people, they didn't count their pennies. And not a scratch on the floor, people like that didn't dance on their heels.

The cabinetmaker stood a little ways off, listening.

"Yes, but what kind of people are they as a rule?" I ask. "Are they business people or military or —?"

"I'm sorry, but I can't tell you that," the landlord

replies. "A closed party, that's all I can say. Speaking about tonight, I don't even know myself — a messenger brought the money."

"It's Flaten," said the cabinetmaker.

"Flaten — really?" asked the landlord, as though he didn't know. "Mr. Flaten has been here before, a fine gentleman, always a fine party. Really? Well, excuse me, I would like to check the hall once more —"

The landlord left.

But the cabinetmaker followed him, asking, "Can't we just watch?"

"What, the dancing? No."

"From a corner or something?"

"No. I don't even allow my wife and daughters, not a soul. The private parties won't stand for it."

"Are you coming or —?" I called, like it was for the last time.

"Yes," the cabinetmaker said, and came.

I asked, "So you knew about this party?"

"Yes," he said. "She mentioned it on Friday."

"Who did? Miss Torsen?"

"Yes. She said I could sit in the gallery."

We continued our walk about town, each with his own thoughts, or both of us with the same thought — anyway I was furious.

"Well, my good Nikolai, I don't think we should

200

buy tickets just to look at Mr. Flaten and his women."

"No."

What a strange idea of Miss Torsen's to invite this man to watch her dancing. It was a trick; but such tricks were like her. Hadn't she taken care to be within earshot of a third party last summer, too, when someone was after her? Something occurs to me, and I ask the cabinetmaker as calmly as I can, "Did Miss Torsen want me to be in the gallery, too, did she say that?"

"No."

"She said nothing about me?"

"No."

I believe you are lying, I thought, she probably also asked you to lie! I was furious, but couldn't squeeze the truth out of the cabinetmaker.

Carriages rumble behind us and stop at "Kronen." Nikolai turned around and wanted to go back, but when he saw me walking on he stopped for just a moment and then came up. I heard him breathe a deep, heavy sigh.

We walked about for about an hour, my anger wore off somewhat and I made myself agreeable to my friend again. We stopped for a beer, went to a movie, and then to a shooting gallery. From there we went to a bowling alley, whiling away the time. Nikolai was the first to call it quits, he looked at his watch and was suddenly in a rush, barely willing to finish the game.

We had to go by "Kronen" again — the carriages were gone. "I knew it!" said the cabinetmaker. He looked crestfallen, he must have wanted to be on hand when the company climbed into their carriages. He peered up and down the street where the carriages had been and repeated, "I knew it!" And now he wanted to go home.

"No, now we're going inside," I said.

*

It was a nice, spacious hall with a bandstand, and a throng of people on the big floor. We sat in the gallery and watched.

There were all sorts of people: sailors, artisans, hotel clerks, salesmen, tramps; so I suppose, considering the circumstances, that the women were everything from seamstresses, servants and shop girls to birds of passage with no daytime occupation. They were dancing lustily. Besides a policeman who would intervene if necessary, the establishment had its own bouncer, with a stick, who strolled up and down the hall keeping an eye on the dancers: at the end of each dance the gentlemen were supposed to step up to the bandstand and pay ten øre. If someone seemed inclined to cheat, the bouncer would give him a friendly tap on the arm with his stick; a gentleman who had to be tapped repeatedly was considered suspect and, as a last resort, shown out. It was remarkably orderly.

Waltz, mazurka, schottisch, rheinlander, waltz —

I noticed a gentleman who danced without a break; tall and with the looks of an Arab, he was very good, a whiz, the ladies flocked to him. Is that Solem lording it down there? I think to myself.

"Aren't you going to dance?" I ask Nikolai, the cabinetmaker.

"Oh no," he says with a smile.

"Then we can leave whenever you wish."

"All right," he says, still sitting.

"You're thinking about something else, aren't you?"

Long pause.

"I was thinking that I don't have a horse on the farm. I haul all the manure and the wood myself."

"That's what has made you so strong."

"I guess I'll have to go home for a few days and get wood for the winter."

"I guess you do."

"What I meant to say," he went on fussily — and fell silent.

"What is it?"

"Well, no, it's out of the question. It would be

nice if you'd come home with me this winter, but. We've got a spare room, nothing much."

"Me? Why? Though I could do worse."

"Oh, if you only would!" said the cabinetmaker.

But now I hear Solem's name down in the hall. Sure enough, there he stands, swaggering, the selfsame Solem from the Tore Peaks. He stands by himself, he's excited — he was the one talking, letting people know he was Solem, the Solem boy. He didn't seem to be with any particular lady, I'd seen him picking them at random as he danced. Then he bowed to the wrong woman, her partner shook his head and said no. Brr! Solem took note. He let the pair dance the next dance, and when the music stopped he approached her again and bowed. And again he was turned down.

The lady was really exceptional — refined or innocent, God only knows. Ash-blond hair, tall, Grecian, in a black dress without trimmings. Oh, how quiet and shy she was! Sure, she was a tart, but so humble, a nun of vice; her face was so pure, suggestive of a pardoned sinner's. A wench like no other!

That was the woman for Solem.

When he got a second no from the gentleman, he began to sound off, acting the Solem boy on the dance floor! But his bravado was tiresome: just wait and see, he would raise a ruckus, all right! It had no oomph, it was familiar prattle to these people. The bouncer wandered over and asked him to pipe down, while pointing at the door where the policeman was taking notice. That calmed the storm, and Solem himself said, "Yes, hssh, let's cut out the racket!" But he didn't lose sight of the Greek lady and her partner.

He let well enough alone for a couple of dances, during which he also danced himself. By now the room was overcrowded, with all the latecomers who'd arrived, and many had to wait their turn for a place on the dance floor, rushing up to be the first next time.

Then something happened.

A couple fell. Solem was one. Getting up, he knocked over another couple, the Greek lady and her partner, there they lay. And, strange to say, Solem was so clumsy getting up that his long arms and legs brought down still another couple. There was a regular pile on the floor, there were screams and curses, indignation and kicks; Solem guided the disaster with a sure hand, with genuine and deliberate malice. Couple after couple tumbled into the pile. The bouncer poked them with his stick, ordering everyone up, the policeman himself came over and the music stopped. Meanwhile Solem had the wise cowardice to wander out the door and be gone.

One by one the fallen got up, rubbing their arms and legs and dusting their clothes, some laughing, some swearing; the partner of the Greek lady had a cut on his temple, he was bleeding and put his hand to his head in a daze. They asked about — what was his name? — that tall fellow who had acted up so. "Solem," some of the women said. There were muttered threats against Solem — oh, it was him all right, someone go find him, he won't get away with it! "But he probably couldn't help it," said the women.

Ah, Solem and women!

But the Greek lady rose from the dust as from a bath. The sand on the floor clung to her black dress, she seemed studded with stars. In her shyness, she had put up with lying at the bottom of the heap, entangled in the legs of other dancers; she just smiled when they showed her that the comb in her Grecian knot was broken.

XXXIII

Forty years ago today, the first of October, we drove the snowplow at home. I'm sorry to say I remember forty years ago.

Nothing escapes me yet, though everything passes me by. I sit in the gallery, watching. If Nikolai the cabinetmaker had been observant he would've seen me crooking my fingers and grimacing, all the more ludicrous for my affectation; luckily he was a child. So I went home, away from it all, and took my seat. My address is Inglenook.

Winter is approaching again, with snow in the North, Anglo-Saxon theater. It'll be an empty time for me, my wheels will come to a standstill, my hair won't grow, my nails won't grow, nothing will grow except my days. And it's a good thing my days grow, from now on it is.

Nothing much happens in the course of the winter — well, Nikolai has gotten an overcoat for the first time. He didn't need it, he bought it for the sake of appearances, he says; and it wasn't cheap, twenty kroner. "But," he adds, "I got it for eighteen!" Nikolai is sure to be happier with his overcoat than Flaten is with his.

By the way, don't let me forget Flaten, something has happened to him: his friends gave him a send-off, celebrating his farewell to bachelorhood with a carouse; he's getting married. It was Miss Torsen who told me this, we met by chance beside her street lamp again and she told me.

"And you're not in mourning?" I asked.

"Oh, no," she said, smiling. "No, it's something

I've known for a long time. And besides, maybe I'm not very constant, I don't know."

"There you hit the mark, I think."

She was taken aback. "How so?"

"You seem to have changed so much since last summer. Then you were straightforward and capable, you saw clearly, you knew what you wanted. What has become of your smattering of bitterness? Or don't you have any reason to be bitter anymore?"

It was much too heavyhanded, but I was like a father and meant well.

She started walking, her head down, pensive. Then she said something very sensible: "Last summer I'd just been fired. I won't mince my words. I'd been given notice, and that, you know, is no laughing matter. It gave me food for thought for a while, that's true. But I don't know — I'm old, but I guess not old enough. I have two sisters who are steady, they're married and capable, though they're younger than I am. I don't know what's wrong with me."

"Would you go to a concert with me?" I asked.

"Now? No, thanks, I'm not dressed." Pause. "But how nice of you to ask!" she said, happy all of a sudden. "It might have been great fun, but — . Instead, let me tell you about that dinner, the party; good grief, the sort of things they dreamed up!"

She was right about that — the merry young fellows had pulled many a mad prank, some childish and stupid, others less so. To begin with, they drank wine of vintage 1812. No, first of course they sent Flaten an invitation; it was in the form of a picture, a broad-minded framed painting with only the time and place and the following: Babel, Bachiad, Offenbachiad, Bacchanal. Then there were speeches for the one who was leaving them, and all the while a deafening chatter over their glasses. And then there was music, some of them were playing the whole time. But as the night wore on this didn't suffice; masked girls appeared and performed some dances, but the champagne had been flowing freely and things got out of hand, so the girls had to go. At that point the gentlemen went down into the hotel entrance to scout for "chance encounters." Aha! — a young woman comes by carrying a child and a bundle of clothes, and with the snow coming down in big wet flakes, she shields the child by bending over it as she walks. "Whoa!" say the gentlemen, catching her, "is it your child?" Yes, it was. "Is it a boy?" — "Yes." They go on chatting with her, she was young and thin, doubtless a servant girl. And they all inspect the lad; Helgesen and Lind, who were nearsighted, polished their glasses so they could see. "Are you off to drown the boy?"

someone asks. "No!" says the girl, bewildered. That was a nasty question, say the others; and the first one agreed it was, and so he fetched his raincoat and draped it over the young girl. Then he chucked the boy under the chin and got him to smile — a wonder of a child, human being and rags and dirt in one bundle. "Poor bastard," he said, "born to a virgin!" "That's better!" the others said. "Now we'll do something," they said. "Where do you live?" they asked the girl. "I used to live at such-and-such," she answers. "*Used to!* Okay, here's what we'll do," one says, taking out his pocketbook. The others do the same and it comes to quite a bundle, it finds its way into the girl's hand. "Wait a minute, stop, I should give her more, I was so nasty," one says. "Me too," the others say, "we were thinking the same as you, let's put down some money for this virgin's son!" A collection is made, with Helgesen as cashier. Then Bengt calls a cab, invites the girl to climb in and then climbs in himself. "It'll just take a moment, I'm only going to Lange Street!" he cries. "Bengt is taking the kid home to his own mother," the others say. It grew quiet after this. "Your eyes are so ridiculously damp, Bolt; how can you cry over those pennies!" "Look to yourself," Bolt answers, "you're melting like an old woman!" Merriment returned, more "chance encounters" occurred. A peasant came along with a cow, headed for the butcher's. "How much do you want for letting our guest take a ride on your cow?" asked young Rolandsen. The peasant smiled and shook his head. So they bought the cow and paid for it. "But wait a minute!" they said. They put a label on the cow and wrote the address of a lady they knew. "Take it to this address," they told the peasant. By the time that was done, Bengt was back again. "Where have *you* been?" they asked, surprised. "The old lady said yes," were his only words. "Hurrah!" they all cried, "and let's drink to the lad! Look, we'll go into the café! Did she really say yes? Hurrah for the old lady too! What are we standing here for, let's walk over to the café!" "*Walk!*" someone says scornfully. "All right, we'll drive, ha-ha-ha — waiter, motorcars, please!" A waiter runs in to telephone. It takes a while, it's getting late, but the gentlemen go on waiting. It's already closing time, people are streaming out of the café. Finally the motorcars appear, a fleet of ten, one apiece. The gentlemen get in. "Where to?" ask the drivers. "Next door," they say. And the ten cars drove to next door, to the café in the same building, and the gentlemen got out and solemnly paid their fares. The café was closed. "Should we break in?" they said. "Of course!" they said. They went at it one and all and bang! the door burst open. The night watchman rushed out shouting — they gathered him up, patted him and hugged him, dived into the cupboards and fished out bottles for him and for themselves, drank and shouted hurrah for the lad, for Bengt's mom, for the lad's mom, for the night watchman, for love and life. When they were done they smacked some banknotes on the watchman's lips and tied them in place with a handkerchief. Then they went back to the hall again. Supper arrived, Flaten's plate was a red silk slipper lined with bottled goods. They ate and drank and caroused for all they were worth, time flew, morning approached, and Flaten began to distribute mementos to them all. One got his watch, another his pocketbook — it was empty — a third his tie pin. Then the turn came for his shoes, one apiece, and he gave his trousers to one and his shirt to another — till Flaten sat naked. They swaddled him in quilts, red silk quilts that they fetched from the hotel rooms. Flaten went to sleep and the nine others kept watch. He slept for an hour, it was morning, they woke him; he jumped out of the quilts, naked, and sent a messenger home for fresh clothes. And the shindig started all over again. . . .

Afterward we talked a bit about Miss Torsen's account; she also added a few things she had forgotten in the telling. She ended by saying, "Anyway, it turned out well for the girl with the child."

"And for the child," I said.

"True. But have you ever heard of such a thing? Poor old lady who ended up with it!"

"You may come to feel differently about that some day."

"Oh? Anyway, it would've been far better if *I* got the money they collected."

"You'll also feel differently about that."

"How so? When?"

"When you get a smiling little boy yourself."

"Oo, don't say such things."

She must have misunderstood me, she was childishly offended. To mollify her, I asked offhand, "And what sort of food did they have at the party?"

"I don't know," she replied.

"You don't know?"

"Heavens, no, I wasn't there," she said, very much surprised.

"No, of course not. I just thought —"

"So that's what you thought, well, well!" she said, even more hurt. And she folded her hands and pried them open again, as she did last summer.

"No, listen, I assure you. I just thought you might have a housewife's interest in the matter. After all, you're taking cooking classes these days."

"Oh, you're just trying to keep me entertained, suiting your words to my interests, aren't you?" Pause. "Well, you're right to a degree, I should have asked about the food, but I forgot."

She appeared to be very irritable this evening. I wondered if Flaten would interest her. Half afraid, I said, "But you haven't told me whom Flaten is marrying."

"She's not attractive in the least," she replied suddenly. "Why do you want to know? You don't know her."

"I suppose Flaten will become a partner in his father's business now?" I went on.

"Oh, that accursed Flaten! You seem to care more for him than I do. I've no idea whether Flaten and Flaten and Flaten will become a partner in his father's business or not."

"I just thought, now that he's getting married —"

"But she's rich too. No, I don't think he'll become his father's partner. He wanted to publish a paper, he told me once. What is there to laugh at?"

"I wasn't laughing."

"Sure you were. Anyway, Flaten wants to publish a paper. And since Lind publishes a 'Doggy News,' Flaten would like to publish a 'People News,' he said."

"A 'People News'?"

"Yes. You should subscribe to it," she said suddenly, straight to my face.

She was obviously at this moment worked up over something I didn't understand, so I didn't answer. I just said, "Should I? Yes, maybe I should." Then she started to cry.

"Dear child, don't cry, I won't pester you anymore."

"You're not pestering me."

"Yes, I am, with my clumsy talk, I can't find the right words."

"No, no, keep talking — it's not that — I don't know —"

What should I talk about? But since, after all, nothing is as interesting as questions about oneself, I said, "You're upset about something, it'll be sure to pass. It must have — not all at once, but it must have affected you nonetheless that . . . well, that he's saying goodbye to you. But remember —"

"You're mistaken," she said, shaking her head, it really doesn't bother me; I had a crush on him once, that's all."

"You also said he was the only one."

"Oh, you know it can seem that way sometimes. But I've certainly been in love with others, I won't deny it. No, Flaten was just being nice, he took me

215

on an outing once and then to a dance, that sort of thing. And, of course, I was flattered that he acknowledged me even though I'd been fired. I think I could have gotten a job in his father's business, but. I'm looking for a job these days."

"You are? I hope you'll find a good one."

"That's just it. But I can't find anything. I mean, I'm sure to find something, but. Like, you know, working in Flaten's store, but that's not for me."

"Poor pay too, I suppose?"

"I think so. And then — I don't know, I somehow know too much for that sort of thing. That accursed degree of mine is doing me nothing but harm. Well, now we won't talk any more about me, it must be late, I have to go."

I walked her to her door, said good night and headed home. I thought and thought, what with the wintry weather, damp streets and absence of sky. No, she was even unfit to get married; no man can be satisfied with having a wife who is only a student. Why doesn't someone in this country realize what is wrong with our young women! Miss Torsen's account of the bash showed once again how she had been groomed to sit and learn and then repeat reams of stuff. She had done real well and forgotten very little, but what she emphasized were the drolleries. I'd been entertained by an eternal schoolgirl, an adult who had wasted her life on learning.

When I got to my door Miss Torsen was there as well; she'd been right on my heels the whole way, as I could tell by the fact that she wasn't the least out of breath when she spoke.

"I forgot to apologize to you," she said

"Dear —?"

"Yes, for saying what I did. You shouldn't subscribe. I'm sorry, please forgive me."

She took my hand and shook it.

In my embarrassment I started jabbering: "That was very witty, 'People News,' ha-ha. Don't stand there getting cold, put your gloves back on. You're going?"

"Yes. Good night. Forgive me for the whole evening."

"Let me walk you home, wait a minute —"

"No, thanks."

Having squeezed my hand hard, she walked away.

She probably wanted to spare my aging legs. The hell with them! But I sneaked after her anyway to see that she got home safely.

＊

Then it happens that Josephine, the workhorse at Tore Peak, comes to town. I met her too, she came to see

217

me — she had looked me up, and once again I flirted with her and called her Josephkin.

How were they doing at Tore Peak? Well, she thanked me on behalf of everyone for asking but shook her head about Paul. He didn't drink so much now, to be sure, but he didn't do anything else either, his will to work had finally snapped. He wanted to sell. He would try to start with a horse and buggy over in Stordalen. I asked if he had a buyer. Yes, Einar, one of the cotters, was eager to get the farm. It was now up to Mr. Brede, who was holding the big mortgage.

I remember her father, the old man from another world, the one with the mittens who had to be fed on gruel because he was ninety years old — I mean the one who smelled so, the living corpse — I remember him and ask Josephine, "I suppose your old father is dead now."

"No, thank God, Father is better than expected. We have to be grateful as long as he can be up and about."

I took Josephine to the movies and the circus, and it was all wonderful. But it was too bad the women rode half naked! Then she wanted to look into one of the big churches, and this she did by herself. She remained in town for a few days and purchased various things; I never saw her pensive or depressed about anything. Then one day she said goodbye, she was going home the next morning.

So she was leaving?

Yes, she had done what she came for. She had also been to see Miss Torsen and gotten the money owed by the actor, because he had never sent anything, of course. "Poor Miss Torsen, she became quite upset that it still wasn't paid, and ashamed and red too. It didn't look like she was doing all that well either, she asked me to wait till the next day, but then I got the money." So now Josephine had nothing more to do in town. At this moment she came from Miss Palm, whom she had visited, but she hadn't been able to see her brother, Nikolai, who was learning cabinetmaking. And it was all one to her, Josephine said, for the last time she had talked to him nothing came of it anyway. So that was that. She wasn't the begging type, she had both a bit of money and some livestock. And if need be, a few pounds of wool — and two bedsteads with linen and everything, she was happy to say — and she wasn't naked either, she was fully equipped, with many changes of both underclothes and overclothes. And besides she was setting up a loom —.

Surprised, I asked if they had been engaged, I

hadn't heard anything.

No, but . . . No, not engaged like with a ring or banns. But they had meant to some day. How else could that sister of his, Sophie Palm, the teacher, have come and lived with them at Tore Peak free of charge for the last two years, acting like some fine lady? But no thank you, no more of that. But again she, Josephine, had certainly thought so once, but it was probably for the best, an act of Providence; it would have been nothing but misery in any case, so that was that.

Suddenly she checked herself. "Oh, good heavens — let me not forget to buy some indigo. For my loom. It was lucky I thought of it. Well, thanks for everything!"

XXXIV

It's during the half holidays the week after Christmas, I've gone home with Nikolai. Since the shop in town is closed anyway, he has taken the time to make this trip and get wood from the forest.

They have a big house. Already Nikolai's father added to the old building, and now Nikolai himself has raised the roof, so there are two floors. He has plenty of space for me, I have a room of my own.

His mother is able and straightforward; she tends to the animals and spends much time washing something or other, even if it's just a used sack. And then she cooks on the stove and keeps her pots and pans sparkling. She's very cleanly: for example, she strains the milk through a sieve lined with a piece of haircloth and rinses the cloth in two waters afterward. But she pokes the dirt from between the tines of her forks with a hairpin.

On the living-room walls hang a mirror, pictures of the German Kaiser's family, a crucifix, and two shelves with a hymnal and a book of sermons, among other things. Folks are still simple and orthodox around here. Everything else in the living room, chairs and table and pedestal and an ingenious chest, Nikolai has made himself.

Nikolai is just as slow and silent here as he was in town, the day after we got here he went off to the woods without a word to his mother. When I asked about him she answered, "I saw him getting the sledge ready, so he must've gone to the woods."

His mother's name is Petra. I don't think she's much over forty, judging by her looks — she too a bit ruddy and big-boned, with fair skin and thick graying hair, a perfect mane. She has a pair of eyes to match the hair, dark eyes, a little tired now, but still pretty good for taking a long, shrewd look over the fjord. Like all the peasants around here, she is taciturn, preferring to keep her big mouth shut.

I ask how long she has been a widow, and it has been almost a generation — "no, I shouldn't turn liar," she says, "but my Sophie in town is twenty-four now, and it was the year after she was born that my husband died." They had only been married a couple of years. Nikolai is twenty-six.

I sit pondering this account, but being old and incompetent, I can't figure it out.

Petra was very proud of her children, especially of Sophie who had gone to school and gotten her degree and now had such an important position. True enough, her whole inheritance had been used up, but she had an education. No one could take that from her. A big, handsome girl Sophie was, there was her picture.

I said I knew her from the Tore Peaks.

"Really, from the Tore Peaks?" Sure, she used to go there in the summer to be with her peers more often, there was nothing wrong with that. But she dropped by at home every year, without fail. "Really, at the Tore Peaks?"

I sometimes go with Nikolai and help out a bit when he's hauling wood. He's strong as a horse and almost indifferent to pain — a cut, a black eye, never mind. And it also turns out that his head can work to good purpose: he ought to have a horse, sure, but he can't keep a horse without getting more fodder. And he won't be able to increase his tillage until he has the wherewithal. Right now he was in town to brush up on his trade, and when he came back he would start making money. Then he would have a horse.

I spent a little time with the neighbors too; the farms were small but the folks raised what they needed and there was no poverty. There were no flowerpots in the windows or pictures on the walls as in Petra's house, but good, thick sheepskin blankets embroidered with old Norwegian designs hung in the farmyards, and the children looked strong and well fed. The neighbors knew very well I was staying with Petra, anyone passing through put up there; it had been that way as long as they could remember. I sensed no hostility toward Petra in these silent people, but the old schoolteacher, who talked more readily, wasn't afraid to gossip about her. This man was a bachelor, but he had his own little house and took care of himself. I wonder if the good gentleman hadn't had a hankering for Petra, the widow, at some time.

The schoolteacher gossips. It was the same with Petra's parents too, anyone passing through put up at their place. There was a spare room and an upstairs, that's where the engineer who laid out the big road stayed, that's where the itinerant lay preachers stayed, and most important, that's where all the peddlers who came around all year stayed. This went on for years, the children grew up, Petra became big and strong. Then along came Palm, he was Swedish, a big trader, a merchant for those days, so to speak; he had his own boat and even a young fellow to do his carrying. And then, you know, panes were seen again in the windows at Petra's parents' and meat appeared on the table on Sundays, for Palm liked to show off; he gave Petra both sweets and dress materials. Then her time was drawing near and Palm went to trade elsewhere. But it so happened that Petra had a boy, and when Palm came back and got to see the boy, he stuck around and didn't travel anymore. They got married, Palm added two rooms to the house, he must have meant to start a shop there; but just when the construction was over and done with, he died. The widow was sitting there with two little ones, but she was well off, Palm was loaded. So why didn't Petra get married again? Though the children were small and a great handicap, she could certainly have found someone, since Petra was still very young. But ever since childhood, the schoolteacher says, she had developed an inclination to take in those tramps and Swedes and peddlers, and so she disgraced herself. Some of them lived there for weeks, eating and drinking and doing nothing and going nowhere. Too shameful for words. And her parents — to their dying day they saw nothing wrong with it, they were used to it and, you know, made some money from it, and so the years went by. Later, when her children were grown and Sophie moved out, she could certainly have gotten married, because she still had half of her assets and was childless to boot, so it was not too late. But no, Petra didn't want to, it was too late, she said — now it was the children's turn to marry, she said.

"I see. Anyway, she must be getting on now?" I remark.

"Yes, time flies," the teacher replies. "I don't know if anyone has tried this year, but there were some last year — there was one — they say. So I hear. But Petra didn't want to. I haven't the foggiest idea what she's waiting for."

"She probably isn't waiting at all."

"Well, it's all the same to me," the schoolteacher says. "But, you see, she puts up all these travelers and tramps and carries on to her heart's content and is an offense to all good Christians. . . ."

Walking home from the schoolteacher's I had

gained a little more insight into the account that
Petra had given me.

*

Nikolai has gone back to the shop in town again, but
I'm staying behind. It doesn't matter where I am, the
winter deadens me anyway.

To keep busy I carefully survey the piece of land
Nikolai will clear when he has the necessary means,
calculating what it will cost with drainage and all —
a scant two hundred kroner. Then he can feed a horse.
It would be a good deed to give him those few kroner, if his mother couldn't. And the country would
have another bit of meadow.

"Look, Petra, why don't you give Nikolai those
two hundred kroner, then he could feed a horse."

"And then four hundred for the horse," she
mumbles.

"That makes six."

"I don't have very many six hundred kroner."

"But couldn't he breed a horse?"

Pause.

"He'll have to clear the land himself."

There was nothing new to me in this way of thinking, one and all have their own problems to struggle
with, Petra has hers. But the strange thing is that they

all struggle as though they still have a hundred years ahead of them.

I used to know two brothers, the Martinsens, they had a big farm and sold produce; they were rich bachelors both of them with no direct heirs. But they were both tubercular, the younger even worse than the older. Then one spring the younger became bedridden for good. He was done for, but he was still interested in everything on the farm. When he heard an unfamiliar voice in the kitchen he called his brother in. "What's up?" he asked. "Just someone wanting to buy eggs." — "What are they a dozen now?" — "Such and such." — "Then give him the smallest ones," he said. A few days later he was dead. The brother lived on, he was sixty-seven and tubercular. Whenever someone came and wanted to buy eggs, he gave them the smallest ones. . . .

"But," I go on to Petra, "it won't pay for Nikolai to clear the land himself, will it? He can make more working at his trade, can't he?"

"Folks here won't use a cabinetmaker anymore," Petra answers. "They buy their tables and chairs at the store, it's cheaper."

"So why is Nikolai getting apprenticed?"

"I've asked the same thing," she answers. "Nikolai just wants to be a cabinetmaker, but it won't amount

227

to anything. Well, let him do what he likes."

"What should he take up instead?"

Pause. Petra's big mouth is shut. Finally she says, "There's a lot of traffic and plenty of tourists in the summer now, both at the Tore Peaks and down here at Nesset. At one time two Danes were staying here, they'd come on foot. 'You should've had a horse and picked us up,' they told me."

Of course, I think to myself, here it comes!

"'You've got a big house and four rooms,' the Danes said, 'high mountains and deep forests,' they said, 'fish in the fjord and fish in the stream, all sorts of things, a wide road,' they said. Nikolai was there and heard it all. 'We managed to get here, but we can't get away again,' they said, 'we have to walk.'"

For something to say, I ask, "Four rooms — are there more than three?"

"Yes, the workshop could be fixed up too," the big mouth answers.

Sure, why not! I thought. And acting on the spur of the moment, I remark, "But if Nikolai is going to drive tourists, he'll need a horse, won't he?"

"We would've found a way somehow," Petra says.

"That's four hundred kroner."

"Yes," she says, "and another hundred and fifty for the carriage."

"But he can't feed a horse!"

"How do the others feed their horses?" she asks. "At Nesset they buy a sack of oats."

"That's eighteen kroner."

"No, seventeen. Which they recover on the first trip."

Ah, Petra had it all figured out, she was a born landlady raised in a boarding house. She can even cook, she puts two strings of macaroni in the barley soup! The money from coffee, from the beds, from the morning waffles had become so dear to her that she put it away, amassing it, growing rich on it. She didn't produce anything the way other countrywomen did — well, nobody can do everything at once, Petra was a parasite. She didn't want to earn a living, she wanted to live off the earnings of tourists who could afford to come.

Oh sure, Anglo-Saxons and grandeur will find their way here too. If all goes well. And it probably will.

*

It's February. Something crosses my mind, a stray thought that just comes to me, and I pick it up; now that the snow is light and crusted over, I'll take my chances and cross the mountains over to Sweden. I'll do it.

But before this can happen I have to wait for some washing, and Petra, who is cleanly, washes in many waters. So I while the time away in Nikolai's workshop, among all sorts of planes and saws and drills and a lathe, making quaint things. For the neighbor's little boys I make a windmill that turns in the wind. It rattles and hums so nicely; from my childhood I remember that these contraptions had an onomatopoeic name: whirligig.

However, I also spend time outdoors, wandering about and using my wintry head as best I can. Nothing comes of it. I don't blame the winter for it, I don't blame anything, but no red irons will come of it, and as for youth and omnipotence — oh God, no! I walk for hours along a path in the woods, my hands on my back, an old man; a memory may brighten my inner landscape awhile, I stop, raise my eyebrows and look ahead in wonder. Would an iron come of it? No, nothing will come of it, it will evaporate, I'm left behind in wistful silence.

But to be young again I pretend to feel a sublime urge — ho, the moment is by no means wasted, images arise, a snatch of flute music:

We came from the heath
from the soft heather,

we came from friendship
and tu-lulu-lu.
A starlet saw us,
two lips meeting,
there just was nothing
as good as you.

Those youthful days,
those happy days,
unlike all others —
now nothing's new.
Then swarmed the bees,
then played the swans,
now no one plays.
But tu-lulu-lu.

I break off and stick the pencil in my pocket while
a note still lingers in me. Then I have at least a bit of
aftertaste.

*

There is a letter for me — well, who can track me
down even here? The letter reads:

Forgive me for writing to you, I would like
to talk to you about something that has hap-

pened. Could I see you when you come back to town? There's nothing the matter. Please don't say no.

Yours,
Ingeborg Torsen

I read it over and over. Has something happened? But I'm off to Sweden, I'm going to bestir myself a bit and not only be wrapped up in other people's business. Do they imagine I've become mankind's old uncle, to be summoned hither and yon for advice! Sorry, I think to myself, playing hard to get and holding my ground, the roads are just right now, I've planned a long trip, a business trip you might say, it means a lot to me, a great deal at stake. . . . How complex the human mind is: as I sit here jabbering to myself, even speaking an angry word out loud now and then so Petra will hear it, I'm not at all displeased to have received this letter; secretly I'm so glad that I find it embarrassing. It was because I would get to see the city again, the frozen gardens, the ships.

But what is it all about? Has she been to see my landlady and gotten my address? Or did she run into Nikolai?

I left immediately.

XXXV

My landlady is surprised. "Oh, good evening! How happy and healthy you look! Your mail is all there."

"Just don't bother. Mrs. Henriksen, you are a gem."

"Ha-ha-ha."

"Yes, you are. And you are a good person. But you gave my address to someone."

"God knows I didn't."

"Ah well, then it wasn't you who did it. Yes, you're right, I'm happy, and tomorrow I'll get up early and walk down to the docks."

"But I did send for someone just now," says my landlady, "maybe I did wrong? A lady, she wanted to know as soon as you arrived."

"A lady, eh? You just sent for her?"

"A little while ago, when you arrived. She certainly was a lovely young lady, she could easily have been your daughter."

"Thanks."

"Well, I really mean it. She would come right away, she said, because she had to talk to you."

The landlady left.

So, Miss Torsen was coming tonight, something must be up. She'd never been in my place before; I looked around — everything nice and tidy. I wash

233

and get ready, that will be her chair; I light the other lamp, too. Now is a good time to read my mail, it will look good; and if I put letters with small feminine handwriting on top, maybe it would make her a little jealous, heh-heh. Good grief, ten or fifteen years ago you could play these games, now it's too late. . . .

She knocked and came in.

I didn't hold out my hand, nor did she, but I offered her the chair.

"Forgive me for being in such a hurry," she said. "I got Mrs. Henriksen to send word; but it's nothing serious and now I'm embarrassed about it, but — ."

I could tell it *was* something serious and my heart began pounding. Why should it pound?

"This is the first time you've been in my place," I say, expectant and deprecating at once.

"Yes. It's very nice," she says without looking around. She began interlacing her fingers and pulling them apart again, making the tips of her gloves slip way out. She was terribly nervous.

"Now I've done something you will approve of, haven't I?" she says, pulling off a glove.

She was wearing a ring.

Good. It didn't sink in right away, only later. I merely asked, "Are you engaged?"

"Yes," she said. She smiled at me, but her lips

were trembling.

I looked back at her and said something like, "Well, look at that!" I nodded paternally and bowed, "Congratulations then!"

"Oh yes, it came to that," she says, "I believe it was the best thing to do. Maybe you think it's fickle or frivolous of me — well, don't you?"

"Not that I know."

"But it was absolutely the best thing to do. I just wanted to tell you."

I got up and she jumped, she was that nervous. But I only got up to fix the lamp behind her, it had started to smoke.

Pause. When she said nothing more, what could I say? But as time dragged on and I saw she was distressed, I asked just the same, "And why did you want to tell me about it?"

"I see what you mean."

"Maybe you thought for a moment that you were the center of the world again?"

"Perhaps."

She looked around with large, flickering eyes and stood up, she'd been sitting on the edge of her chair the whole time. I stood up too. An unhappy woman, I could see that much, but good God, what could I do? Here she came telling me she was engaged and looking very unhappy, was that a way to behave! But now that she stood up I could see her more clearly under her hat — her hair! Silky, silvery hairs were appearing at her temples, it was so beautiful. She is tall and lovely, her bosom rises and falls, she has such a high bosom, ah, such a high bosom, rising and falling, look. And her face is high-colored, her mouth open, her parted lips dry, feverishly dry — .

"Miss Ingeborg," I say, calling her that for the first time. And I reach slightly toward her, wanting to touch her maybe, to stroke her, no, I don't know — .

But now she has collected herself, she stands upright, radiant. Her eyes have cooled, they look at me, putting me in my place again as she walks to the door.

I blurt out, "No —!"

"What is it?" she asks.

"Don't go, not yet, not right away, sit down again and tell me more."

"No, you're perfectly correct," she says, "I'm not the center of the world. Here I come to you with my trifles, to you who — just look at your mail from all over the world."

"Now listen, sit down again, I won't ever read that mail, it's nothing, maybe two or three letters, and they're probably from complete strangers. Just sit down and tell me everything, you owe me that. Look, I won't even read the mail."

With that I gathered up all the letters and threw them onto the fire.

"Good heavens, what are you doing!" she cries out, running to the rescue.

"Don't bother," I say. "I don't expect to receive any joys by mail, and I don't look for trouble."

Now that she was standing so near I was on the verge of touching her again, for just a moment, touching her arm; but I caught myself and forbore. I'd probably gone too far already, so I said kindly and sympathetically, because I felt so sorry for her, "Dear child, you mustn't be so unhappy, everything will be all right, you'll see. Just sit down — thank you, that's right."

She seemed so surprised by my emotion that she sank down in her chair again, as though in a daze. She said, "I'm not unhappy."

"No? Good!" And now I rattle away, while trying to hold back and just play uncle to her. I talk to distract her, to distract *us*, jabbering away, I can hear the buzz of our voices. What could I say? Nothing and everything, lots.

"All right, my child. And who is the man you're giving your hand to — and who's giving his hand to you — who is he? It was nice of you to come to me first, I realize that now, thank you. You see, I just got home and I didn't sleep much along the way; I was in suspense — well, not suspense, but anyway I was — you know what it's like traveling by steamer, lots of people, rattling chains, brr, so I didn't sleep much. Then I got home and here you are, and thank you, Miss Ingeborg — I'm a father and you're a young child, so I call you Ingeborg. But when you told me all this I hadn't slept, I was off balance — I didn't have the right perspective, to give good advice, I mean. But now you can rest assured, I would really like to know: Is he old? Young? Of course young. I'm sitting here wondering how you will get along, Miss Ingeborg, in those unknown circumstances, I mean; I suppose it will be quite different from what you're used to maybe, but God bless you, you'll get along fine, I'm sure —"

"But you don't know who it is?" she breaks in, looking anxiously at me again.

"No, I don't, and there's no need to tell me right now if you'd rather wait. Who it is? A fine little man, I can tell that by the ring, a teacher maybe, a clever young teacher?"

She shakes her head.

"Then a big, good-natured fellow who will dance with you —?"

"Maybe," she says softly.

"There you see, I got it. A bear who can lift you in his paws. On your birthday — do you know what he'll give you for your birthday?"

But now I was probably becoming too childish, boring her; for the first time she looked at a picture on the wall and then at another. But it wasn't so easy for me to stop, I had barely spoken for several weeks and was overexcited too boot. God knows why.

"How was it in the country?" she suddenly asks. Since I have no idea what she's getting at and merely look at her, she goes on, "You were at Nikolai's mother's, weren't you?"

"Yes."

"What's she like?"

"Does she interest you?"

"Well, maybe not. Oh, dear me!" she says wearily. "Really now, is that the right tune for someone newly engaged! How it was in the country? Well, there was a schoolteacher, you know, an old bachelor, sly as they come, grand. He said he knew me and put on airs the first day; as for me, I told him I came solely to see him. 'That's utterly impossible!' he said. 'Why?' I said. 'You've been a schoolmaster for forty years, you're a respectable man, a faithful churchgoer, chairman of the community board, the big boss.' I sat in on one of his classes. Splendid; the teacher talked the whole time — of course he had an audience that day, it was like an inspection: 'You, Peder! Hmm. A horse and a man came along, one was riding on the other's back, who was riding, Peder?' — 'The man!' Peder replied. Pause. 'You're quite right, Peder, it was the man who did the riding. And so it is with sin, it's Satan riding us.'"

But now she was looking at the walls again, I seemed to be losing her once more. I tried an oblique tack: "You'd probably rather hear about people you know, about the Tore Peaks, say. Josephine was here."

"Yes," she said, nodding.

"Do you remember the old fellow at the Tore Peaks? I don't think I'll ever forget him. In so and so many years, I'll be like him — in not so terribly many years! I'll be a child again, from old age. He came out once, made his way down to the field, I saw him, he had mittens on. You know, he would eat anything — he sat there munching hay."

She stared at me idiotically.

"True, he did look like he'd never been given hay before. It could be because it had gone bad, of course. It was the hay that had been left out, you know, the stuff that had been left to rot till next year, the next tourist season."

"You must think you need to cheer me up," she says smiling, "that I'm deeply unhappy. On the contrary. He's really too good for me; at least his sister must think so, since she's been against me. But it will be a pleasure to ignore that sister. Anyway, I'm not unhappy, that's not why I've come. I certainly would rather have him than anyone else — if I can't have the one I want."

"Child, you said that once before — yes, you mentioned it last winter. But, you know, the one you want is gone, isn't he? And besides you seemed to feel that you weren't right for him, or that he wasn't right for you, I mean —"

"Right? I'm not right for anyone! Do you think I'm right for where I'm going? I'm afraid I haven't turned out right for anyone at all, I don't know who on earth it would be. But the question is whether I can carry it off, whether he can put up with me. But I'll do my very best, that I've promised myself."

"So who is it? Do I know him? You're not right for him? That's funny. Of course, he'll be very fond of you, crazy about you in fact, and you'll love him in return. Listen, Miss Ingeborg, you will carry it off brilliantly, you're capable and intelligent —"

"Oh well!" she said sullenly, getting up. But then she hesitated, started to say something but changed her mind. Finally she went up to the door and, turning away from me and tugging at her gloves, she asked, "So you think I should do it?"

I was extremely surprised by the question and said, "Do it? Haven't you done it?"

"Oh yes. That is — yes, I've done it, I'm engaged. And what you've been saying all this time shows that I've done the right thing."

"Well, I'm not so sure, I can't possibly know that," I replied, going up to her. "Who is it, then?"

"Oh God, never mind, I can't take it anymore. Good night."

She fumbled for my hand, but as she was looking at the floor she couldn't find me, our hands kept missing one another, and she opened the door and was gone. I called to her, asking her to wait a minute, then I grabbed my hat and hurried after her. The stairs were empty. I went all the way down and opened the street door — the street was empty. She must have run.

I'll try to see her tomorrow, I thought.

*

One day, two days, I didn't see her, though I went to her usual haunts. Another day — no. Then I decided to go to her home and ask. At first I thought there would be nothing strange about that, but when the chips were down I changed my mind. You always lose something when you make a fool of yourself. But wasn't I the uncle? No — yes, of course, but still.

A week passes, two weeks, three — she seems to have vanished. Surely there couldn't have been an accident! I climb the stairs and ring her bell.

She's already gone, they left as soon as they were married, last week. She has married Nikolai, Nikolai the cabinetmaker.

*

March — oh, what a month! Winter is over, but there is no telling in March how long it may linger. That's what the month of March is for.

I've lived through another winter and seen the blessed trumpery offered in the Anglo-Saxon theater. You were up there too, my little friend, you saw how good we were at performing tricks, you were part of it yourself in fact, you still have a sweet little memory of the rib you cracked. I watched it from a distance, twelve miles off; there were no people nearby, but seven heavens above me.

Soon I'll read what the district governors report about the year's harvest in our country — that is, about the income of Theater Norway — ho, dollars, sterling!

And the jesting professor will cavort in his element. There he comes, smug and confident, Sir Mediocrity in all his majesty. In the coming year he'll recruit more farsighted people and spruce up Norway even more, making Norway still more eye-catching to those Anglo-Saxons. More dollars, more sterling, ho!

What, is someone grumbling?

Switzerland.

Then we'll have to invite Switzerland for dinner and make a speech for it: Colleague, our great goal is to be like you. Who can exploit their Alps the way you do, who can file such watch wheels! Switzerland, make yourself at home, we won't steal you, there are no pickpockets at this table. Skoal!

But if that doesn't help we must stand up and fight; there are still Norwegians in good old Norway, we can compete with — Switzerland.

*

Mrs. Henriksen brings me catkins in a glass.

"What, is it spring?"

"Yes, it won't be long now."

"Then I'll be going. You see, Mrs. Henriksen, I'd be happy to stay, because this is where I really belong, but what more can I do here? I don't work, I just hang around. Can you understand that sort of thing? I fret the whole time, my heart is getting wrinkles. My most brilliant game now is heads or tails: I toss a coin in the air and wait. When I came to you last fall I wasn't that despondent, not at all, and I was only half a year younger; but I was ten years younger. So what has happened to me? Nothing. Only, the person I was last fall no longer exists."

"But you've been chipper all winter. And when you came back from the country three weeks ago you were so happy, weren't you?"

"Was I? I don't remember. No, things don't change that fast, and nothing has happened to me these last three weeks. Well, enough of that; anyway, I'm leaving. When spring comes I leave, I've always done that, and I'll pretend to be the same as I used to be. Sit down, Mrs. Henriksen."

"No, thank you, I don't have time."

"I see, you don't have time. You're working, you're not ten years older; I've noticed it's heavy going for you to rest even on Sundays. Dear Mrs. Henriksen! You and your little daughter knit socks for the family, you take in lodgers, you are a mother and hold the whole family together. Don't let your little Lovise sit for twelve hours at a school desk. If you do, you'll

245

hardly see her during those crucial growing-up years, and she won't take after you and learn from you. She may learn enough to have children, but she won't learn to be a mother, and when she has a home and family herself to hold together, she won't be able to. She'll know only about languages and math and Rolf Bluebeard, but that won't give sustenance to her life as a woman. That means her nature will have to live on a starvation diet for twelve years on end."

"Excuse my asking, but where will you be going now?"

"I don't know, but I'm going. Where? I'll catch a steamer and sail, and when I've sailed a goodly while I'll go ashore. Then, if I look around and see I've gone too far or not far enough, I'll board another ship and sail some more. Once on a tramp in Sweden, I got to Kalmar; when I looked over to Öland, I knew I'd gone too far and turned back. Nobody cares where I am, least of all myself."

XXXVI

One gets used to everything, one gets used to another two years passing.

And now it's spring again.

There is a fair in this border town and my hideaway is getting very noisy; there's music off in the fields, the merry-go-round is whirling, the tightrope walker is babbling in front of his tent, and people of every description stream to and fro in the town. There is a big gathering; a few Norwegians have also crossed the mountain, horses neigh and whinny, cows low, business hums.

In the window of the goldsmith straight across from my hideaway, a big silver cow has turned up these days, oh, a handsome brood cow which the local farmers stop to stare at. "She's too pretty for my mountains," says one, laughing. "I wonder what she costs," says another, laughing. "You want to buy her?" — "No, not enough feed this year."

A man comes lumbering along at an easy pace and also stops in front of the window. I see him from the back, he has such a broad back. He stands there a long time — he must be pondering something, because he scratches his beard from time to time. God help me, there he stomps into the shop; he's not going to buy the silver cow, is he!

It takes an eternity, he doesn't come out again, what's he doing in there? Once I've started keeping an eye on him, I can't do it by halves, so I take my hat and walk across to the goldsmith's window too. I stand there with the others and watch the door.

Then the man comes out again — sure enough, it's Nikolai. It was his back and his hands, but he has grown a beard and looks gorgeous. Just imagine, Nikolai the cabinetmaker here!

We say hello and, taking his time, he gives me his hand; we talk, it's heavy going, but it goes. Yes, of course, he was here on business in a way. "You didn't buy the silver cow, did you?" — "Oh no, not I. No, what I went in about isn't worth mentioning. It came to nothing anyway. . . ." At length he lets me know he is horse trading, he's going to have a horse. And I learn he has cleared his piece of land and is seeding it for a grassplot, and that his wife — er, thanks for asking — is in good health.

"What I meant to say, did you cross the mountain to get here?" he asks.

"Yes, last winter, in December."

"Oh, if I'd known!"

I tell him I couldn't spare the time to drop by then, I was in a hurry, a bit of business —.

"I see," he said.

Not much more is said between us, Nikolai was the same silent man as before. He also has some more business to take care of, and since he can't be gone from the farm for very long, he has to head home tomorrow. "Did you buy a horse?" — "M-no, I didn't." — "The deal won't come off?" — "I don't know. It's a matter of twenty-five kroner, I want him to split fifty-fifty."

Later that day I see Nikolai go into the goldsmith's shop again. That was a lot of coming and going. I could have good company over the mountain now, I think to myself; it's spring, don't I always travel in the spring? I start packing my bag.

Nikolai comes out again looking as empty-handed as he went in. I open the window and ask if he has bought the horse. "M-no, the man won't give." — "So why can't you give instead?" — "Well, sure," he says hesitantly. "It's just that I don't have that much cash." — "I can let you have some on loan." Then Nikolai smiles and shakes his head, as though my offer were a fairy tale. "Thanks anyway!" he says, starting to go. "Where are you going?" I ask. "To look at another horse. It's old and not much, but."

Was I taking too much interest in Nikolai's horse, was I sucking up to the man? Me? Why? I don't understand. He was offended that I had walked past his door last winter, and now I wanted to make it up to him, that's all. But so I wouldn't have anything to blame myself for, I stopped packing my bag and decided not to offer Nikolai my company. Instead I went for a walk in town, which I suppose I could do just like

249

everyone else.

I meet Nikolai in the street with a colt and we swap a few words: "So you bought it?" — "I wound up buying it, sure, the man gave in at last," he replies, smiling.

We both lead the horse to the stable, feed it and stroke it; it's a mare, two and a half, sorrel, with an almost white mane and tail, a little lady.

In the evening Nikolai comes on his own to my hideaway and chats briefly about the mare and the condition of the trail over the mountain. Then he says goodbye and goes to the door. "I've been thinking," he says, "if you won't sneeze at it, that now you could have a ride for your bag. We could be there the day after tomorrow," he adds.

So was I supposed to offend him once again?

*

We walked all day, spent the night at a mountain hut on the border, and walked some more. Nikolai is carrying my bag the whole way, in addition to his own parcels; when I suggest strapping the load to the mare, he says it's nothing much to carry. You see, Nikolai wanted to spare the sorrel lady.

By noon we can see the fjord below us, and Nikolai stops to give the mare another thorough grooming.

As we descend I begin to feel a pressure, a tightening; it's the sea air. Nikolai asks what's up, but it's nothing.

We reach his house. The farmyard is well swept. We can see the derrière of a woman kneeling in the doorway, washing the floor. Today is Saturday.

"Whoa!" cries Nikolai, needlessly loud, and stops.

The woman in the doorway gives a backward glance; her hair is gray but it's her, Miss Ingeborg, Mrs. Ingeborg. "Oh goodness!" she says, giving the floor a couple of quick swipes to finish up.

"Just look at her going at it," Nikolai says playfully. "Now she's in her element!" he says.

And I who thought that Nikolai the cabinetmaker would never crack a joke! Ah, but he'd been so contented the whole way, he was so proud of the lady he was bringing home, and he pats her even now.

Mrs. Ingeborg gets up, her dress wet and dirty. It all seems strange to me, she's so gray, I need a little time, a moment, and I want to give her time too, so I turn away.

"Oh, what a nice horse!" I hear her say.

Nikolai pats and pats. "And I've brought a visitor with me," he says.

I walk up to her, probably overdoing my simplicity a little, I don't know. "Hello," I say, taking the wet hand that she's too embarrassed to give me. Somehow I feel like standing on ceremony with her, I don't let go of her hand but repeat, "Hello! How are you?"

"Oh hello. Good heavens!" she answers.

I go on in the same tone: "Blame your husband, he's the one who dragged me here."

"Welcome," she says. "A good thing I just finished cleaning."

A brief silence; we look at each other, it's been two years. For something to do we all three start inspecting the mare, and Nikolai is ready to burst with pride. Then we hear a child announcing itself from the open door to the living room, and the young mother runs off. "Please come in!" she calls back to us.

As soon as I enter I notice that the living room has changed since the last time I was there. All sorts of middle-class doodads have turned up: white curtains on the windows, several pictures on the walls, a hanging lamp, a round table and chairs in the middle of the floor, knickknacks on a whatnot, a spinning wheel decorated with rose painting, a flower stand — the room is full! These were probably all things Mrs. Ingeborg was used to from her home and thought genteel. All right; but in Petra's day this was a light, spacious room.

"And where's your mother?" I ask Nikolai.

He hesitates, as usual. His wife answers, "Oh, she's doing fine."

But where is she? I wanted to ask, but refrained.

"Look, I would like to show you something," says Mrs. Ingeborg.

It was the child, a boy, big and handsome, just over a year old, a really splendid fellow there in his crib. When he saw me he made a face, but only for a moment; as soon as he was on his mother's arm he looked at me without fear.

Goodness, the young mother was so happy and so beautiful. Can you imagine, her eyes were full of a mysterious tenderness they had never had before.

"What a fine fellow!" I say, boasting of him.

"Ha, I should think so!" the mother says.

*

One gets used to everything: the sea air no longer weighs on me, and I can talk to her who is now mistress of the house without getting winded. And she is also glad to talk, gushing nervously; it seems to be a long time since she opened her mouth. What we talked about? We didn't trade questions and answers about the degrees of the various angles or about Shakespeare's grammar.

Had she ever imagined that her degree would end

up here, in the cow barn or with her doing Saturday cleaning?

Oh, the little freak! She had picked up the ABC's of a dozen subjects, but whenever she met an adult with some common knowledge, she was at a loss. She had other things to think about now, home and family and the animals. Of course, there weren't very many animals at the moment, since Nikolai's mother took half of them along with her — .

"Is Petra gone?"

Married. To the schoolteacher. Petra hadn't wanted to be here once the new wife arrived. One evening there appeared a stranger in the yard, Petra wanted to put him up for the night, Mrs. Ingeborg did not — she knew him and insisted he leave. This led to a disagreement between the old and the new mistress. Besides, Petra thought the young wife was stupid in the cow barn. And in fact, she didn't know very much, but she was learning more and more, it became fun to be good at something. She didn't ask any questions, she knew that would be a mistake, but she thought things out for herself and kept her eyes open when visiting the neighboring farms. Still, there were things she would never learn, she wasn't born to them. The wives of government officials in the country are often from small towns, they haven't grown up with country ways — they learn them, but they never really learn them. They know only so much, what needs to be done from day to day. To set up a loom one must have grown up with the sound of the batten, to tend animals well one must have been around them since childhood, helping one's mother. One can learn this from others, but it won't be in one's blood. And not everyone has a Nikolai beside her! The young wife is so taken with Nikolai, that strong, healthy animal who is, in turn, crazy about her. And besides, Nikolai was so patient, he thought his wife was very capable, wonderful. Of course, she did go to great pains to do well, and it left its mark on her, she had not turned gray for nothing. And now, on top of everything, she had lost a front tooth — here, look — a couple of months ago that was, it got broken on buckshot left in a grouse. She didn't dare look in the mirror anymore, she didn't recognize herself. But it didn't matter as long as Nikolai. . . . Just look what he'd bought her, a brooch, from the goldsmith at the fair, wasn't it pretty? Oh, that Nikolai, what a crazy lad; but in return she would fulfill his every wish. Just imagine, to take from the money set aside for a horse and buy a brooch! "Where is he now, I wonder, where did he go? I bet he's outside patting the mare again, ha-ha!"

"Nikolai!" she called out. Sure, he answered from the stable.

She sat down again, crossing her legs. She was a bit flushed, maybe at some thought, some memory — it made her attractive, she was excited and beautiful. And with her dress clinging to her body, her limbs were clearly outlined under it. She began patting her knee.

"Is the boy sleeping?" I ask, for something to say.

"He's sleeping. Oh, that boy!" she exclaims. "Can you imagine anything so wonderful? You'll have to excuse me, but —. And he's only a little over a year old! I never knew children were such blessings."

"There you can see!"

"Well, I did think differently once, I haven't forgotten, and you disagreed with me. I was stupid, of course. Children? A sheer wonder! And as you get older, the only joy, the last joy. I want to have more of them, many — why, I would like my children to stand beside one another looking like organ pipes, each one taller than the next. They are such a delight. . . . But I have to admit I wish I hadn't lost my tooth, it leaves a black hole. Really, I feel sorry about it, for Nikolai's sake. I could get a new one, but I wouldn't ever; and I hear it's so expensive. And besides, I don't want to play games anymore; if only I'd quit before, but I had my chance too late. Just think of all I missed out on that way, my whole childhood, my whole youth. Even as an adult, didn't I spend my summers loafing around at health resorts! I was supposed to have a vacation from teaching school, to catch my breath, but I sank down into sheer laziness and demeaned myself every day. I could scream with remorse. I could've been married ten years ago and had a home and children and a husband all that time; now I'm old already, cheated of ten years of my life. And my hair is gray, a tooth missing —"

"Now listen, you've lost one tooth, I'll soon have only one left."

But I regretted this as soon as I had consoled her with it. Why should I pretend to be in worse shape than I was? It was bad enough already. Oh, how I vexed myself green, sitting there laughing and grinning to show my teeth — "here, take a look, take a really good look!" I'm afraid she noticed how I was showing off; everything I did was wrong.

Then she consoled me in turn, as people who can afford it do: "You're that decrepit, are you? Ha-ha!"

"Have you met the schoolmaster?" I ask quickly.

"Of course. You remember what you told me about him, don't you? A horse and a man came riding down the road. . . . But he's smart and greedy — oh, he's sly, he borrows our harrow since ours is new and a good one. They've built a house and take in travelers coming up the valley, a big hotel, with maids in native costumes. Oh yes, Nikolai and I were both at their wedding, Petra looked really nice and winsome. You mustn't think Petra and I are on bad terms any longer, she puts up with me more readily now that I'm better at doing things, and last summer they asked me to come over several times to interpret for Englishmen and the like — I know just enough for that. Oh dear! . . . I wouldn't have had a serious falling out with Petra at all, but then Sophie came home — you know, that schoolmistress from town. She'd found so much fault with me before, so I didn't care for her, I freely admit it; but then she came home and was just as high and mighty as ever and acted like she knew everything. I was busy trying to learn how to cope here, and then she came along and set me back, talking about the Seven Years War — she was such an expert on the Seven Years War, she'd taken an exam on it. And then we didn't talk correctly enough for her, Nikolai sometimes said 'ain't' and 'nothin' and that was all wrong. But Nikolai talks fine, why should that ninny, his sister, be putting on airs? And besides, she showed up here and was — well, she'd been engaged, so she had to take a leave for six months. The child is with Petra, the grandmother, so it's doing fine; it's a boy too, but he has almost no hair, mine has lots of hair. Well, it was too bad about Sophie in a way, because she'd spent her inheritance and all those years studying to be a schoolmistress, and then she came home that way. But she was insufferable, letting it be known that at least she hadn't been fired, like me. So I asked her to go. And off they went, both Sophie and her mother. But as I told you, her mother and I have patched things up. Though you mustn't think she helped us buy the horse. Far from it. That money came out of a bank loan. But it'll be all right, it's our only debt. And Nikolai made everything here himself, the table and the whatnot and everything you see, we didn't buy it. He also cleared the big new field down there himself. And we'll have more animals, you should see the new heifer. . . . Oh, you know, not even the food was good enough for Sophie; canned goods were so handy, we should buy canned goods, she said. It was enough to make you sick. I had started knitting, I got one of the neighbors to show me how to do it right, and I was knitting socks for myself. But no, Miss Sophie always bought her socks in town. Oh, she was real sweet. 'Get out!' I told her. And so they moved out. Ha-ha-ha!"

Nikolai comes in. "Did you call me?"

"No — oh yes, I wondered if you could come upstairs with me, I need something to hang things on by the stove, a clothesline; come — ."

I sat there thinking. If only it lasts! She's so high-strung, she feeds on her nerves. And of course she's pregnant again. But how wonderfully strong-willed she is, and how much she has matured these last two years! And what it has cost her too!

Hang tough, child, hang tough!

At least she had vanquished Sophie, the school-marm who had tried to turn Nikolai against her at one time. Out of the house! How gratifying that must have been for Mrs. Ingeborg — that small triumph was priceless. The fact that such things occupied her showed how much her life had changed, she was still excited when she talked about it, tugging at her fingers, a habit from her schooldays. And why shouldn't she feel gratified? A small triumph now ranked as high as a greater one in days gone by. The perspective had changed, but the satisfaction was no less.

Listen — she has begun to read upstairs, a soft murmur is heard. Of course, today is Sunday, and since she is the one with most book learning, it falls to her to read the family prayers. Bravo! Splendid! This too she has disciplined herself to do, for they still stick with tradition around here. Look, you may not be a believer, no, but if you are nothing else either, what are you? You read the prayers. It was quite a nice idea, that clothesline.

She has become an able cook too, in country fashion — the meat soup was delicious, without macaroni but just as it should be, with barley, carrots and thyme. She scarcely learned that in her housekeeping course. I sit here thinking about all she has learned, it's a great deal. Maybe that thing about children like organ pipes was a bit overwrought. Well, I don't know, but her nostrils flared as she said it, she was like a filly. She must have known how reluctant middle-class couples were to have children, how briefly love lasted between them: they stayed together by day to keep people from talking, but spent the night apart. She would turn her home into a house of conception: she and her husband were most often apart by day, each at his or her work, but every night brought them together.

Bravo, Mrs. Ingeborg!

XXXVII

I should really leave now, or I could move over to Petra and the schoolmaster's, where they take in travelers. I really should.

Nikolai has put the sorrel lady to work, hitching her to a nice little cart he has made himself and furnished with iron fittings. And now the lady is hauling manure. There isn't all that much of this commodity on the small farm with its few animals, so it's soon done. Then the lady pulls the plow, stepping along as though she were pulling nothing more than the train of a dress. Nikolai has never heard of such a horse before, nor has his wife.

And now I take a walk on the newly cleared field, looking at it from all sides. I pick up a handful of dirt, thumb it and nod, as if I knew something about the different types of soil. Marl, couldn't be better.

I walk far enough to see the gargoyles on Petra's hotel — but suddenly I turn off the road and up into the woods, to where the ground was bare and to catkins and tu-lulu-lu. Here the air is still, spring is on the way.

And so the day goes by.

I feel very comfortable and happy here, if only I could stay! I would pay very well and make myself profitable and well-liked, I wouldn't hurt a fly. But in the evening I mention to Nikolai that now I had better move on, this won't do. . . . I didn't mind if he passed it on.

"Can't you stick around a little while?" he says. "But I guess we can't offer you all that —"

"Of course you can, God bless you, Nikolai, but still. It's spring, you know, and in the spring I travel; I would have to be really decrepit before giving that up. And besides you're probably tired of me, your wife at any rate."

I didn't mind if he passed this on, too.

Then I pack my bag and wait. No, nobody comes to take the bag out of my hands and forbid me to pack any more. So maybe Nikolai didn't pass anything on — did that man ever manage to open his mouth! Then I slap the bag on a chair in the middle of the floor so it sits there ready-packed, in full sight of everybody, and now we are leaving. I wait till well into the morning the next day, by which time the bag has certainly been noticed, but no. So I have to look out when the mistress calls us for dinner and makes some remark as she points to that thing in the middle of the floor.

"It appears I've taken it into my head to leave today."

"Oh, no. Why?" she answers.

"Why? Well, don't you think I should?"

"Oh yes. But you could've stayed a while longer, because just now the cows are going to pasture and we'll have more milk."

Nothing more was said; she went off.

Bravo, Mrs. Ingeborg! I'll be damned, but you're a shining ducat! It struck me now as it had several times before that there had come to be little difference between her and Josephine at Tore Peak; both in the way they thought and the way they expressed themselves, they were getting more and more alike. Those twelve years of schooling had set no roots in the young girl's mind, though they had certainly loosened many of her own. However that may be, hang tough now!

*

Then Nikolai is going to the trading center, and since he has to bring home flour, he plans to drive. I know full well I ought to go with him, then I could take the packet boat the day after tomorrow; I explain this to Nikolai and pay for my keep. While he's hitching up the horse I pack and repack my things.

Oh, this eternal wandering! Hardly settled in one place before you're unsettled in another, no home, no roots. What are those bells I hear? Ah, Mrs. Ingeborg is letting out the cows! They are going to pasture for the first time, and there will be more milk. . . . There Nikolai comes to say he's ready to go. Okay, the bag's right here.

"Listen, Nikolai, isn't it a bit early to be letting the cows out?"

"Sure. But they won't keep quiet in their stalls anymore."

"I was in the woods yesterday, I wanted to sit down but I can't sit in the snow. No, I can't, though I could ten years ago. I have to wait till there's really something to sit on. A stone is good enough of course, but nobody can sit for long on a stone in May."

Nikolai glances anxiously out the window at the mare.

"Well, let's get going. . . . And there weren't any butterflies either. You know the ones with wings like pansies, there weren't any of those. And if joy dwells in the woods, I mean if God himself — he hasn't moved there yet, it's too early."

Nikolai doesn't say a word to my twaddle. Anyway, it's just a muddled expression of a mood, a faint wistfulness.

We go out the door.

"Nikolai, I'm not going."

He turns around and looks at me, then his eyes smile good-naturedly.

"You see, Nikolai, I think I have an idea, I feel like an idea has just come to me that might turn into a great, red iron. So I can't be disturbed. I'm not going."

"Ah, very good," Nikolai says. "Well, as long as you're satisfied here . . ."

And now, fifteen minutes later, I'm watching Nikolai and the mare ambling down the road. Mrs. Ingeborg stands out in the yard with the boy on her arm, showing him the cavorting cows.

And here stand I. A fine old geezer, I am.

*

Nikolai comes back with mail for me, it has been piling up for weeks.

"But you don't usually read your letters?" Mrs. Ingeborg says playfully. Nikolai is listening.

"Well, say the word and I'll burn them unread," I answer back.

Suddenly she turns pale. She puts her hand on the letters in jest, covering part of my hand as well. I feel a warmth so great, a strange momentary blood-warmth, more than blood-warmth, just a moment, before she withdraws her hand and says, "I suppose we'll spare them."

Now she was a deep red.

"I once saw him burn his mail," she said to Nikolai. Then she went up to the stove and busied herself with something; she asked her husband about the trip, the road, if the mare had behaved herself. She had.

A tiny detail, without importance to anyone. I probably shouldn't have mentioned it.

*

Several days later.

The weather has gotten warm, my window is open, my door to the living room is open, everything is quiet. I'm standing at the window looking out.

A man came into the yard carrying a shapeless bundle. Since I didn't see him clearly, I thought it was Nikolai carrying something, and I sat down at the table again.

A little later I hear someone say hello in the living room.

Mrs. Ingeborg doesn't answer, but I hear her ask in a loud and firm voice, "Why have you come here?"

A strange man's voice answers, "To say hello."

"My husband isn't here, he's out."

"That doesn't matter."

"Yes, it does matter," she cries out, "you must leave!"

I don't know how she looked at that moment, but her voice was somber with tears and agitation. A moment later I was in the room.

The stranger was Solem.

What, Solem here? He was everywhere. Our eyes met.

"Weren't you asked to leave?" I said.

"Take it easy, will you!" he answered, in a sort of semi-Swedish. "I'm in the skin trade now, I go around the farms and buy up hides. Do you have any?"

"*No!*" the woman screams; her voice broke. Quite beside herself, she suddenly pushed a ladle into something bubbling on the stove and might have thrown it —

Then Nikolai walked through the door.

All at once the stolid man came alive, he must have seen at a glance what was up. Did he know Solem, and had he seen him coming? He gave a short laugh, "heh-heh," followed by a frozen smile. It was uncanny — he was so white, and it looked as though his face had been seized with a smiling cramp. Here Solem had met his peer, his macho double, with the strength and spirit of a stallion. And he goes on smiling. "Well, I guess you don't have any hides," Solem says, finding his way to the door. Nikolai goes after him, smiling. Out in the yard he helps put the bundle onto Solem's back. "Thanks!" Solem says, sounding ill at ease. Then Nikolai lifted up the huge load of skins, of hides, and let it down again, let it down oddly, overdoing it, so that Solem's knees buckled and he fell forward. A groan was heard, it hurt, the ground was hard as a rock. Solem stays down for a moment before getting up; he's no longer himself, his face is bruised, blood trickles into his eyes. He tries to push the heavy bundle sideways on his back, but it continues to hang askew; he starts walking anyway, with Nikolai hard on his heels, smiling. They follow the road, one after the other, till they come to the woods, then they vanish from sight.

Well, let us be human — being knocked down was not pleasant. And that heavy load hanging so badly from one shoulder looked painful too.

Then I hear sobbing in the living room, Mrs. Ingeborg has collapsed in a chair. In her condition!

Well, it takes its time, but it gets better, it passes; we start to talk a bit, I ask her little questions and get her to compose herself.

"He, that man — that hired hand — you have no idea how awful he is, I'll kill him! He was the one who — he was the first one; but now he'll get what's coming to him, and more, you'll see. He was the first one, I was decent till then, but then he became the first. And it didn't even mean very much to me, I won't pretend to be any better than I am, it seemed pretty unimportant; but later it was brought home to me. And it led to so much that was bad, I sank so low, to my knees. It was his fault. And later, as I said, everything was brought home to me. For heaven's sake,

269

I want to be let alone by that man, I don't want to set eyes on him ever again! Do you think that's asking too much? But Nikolai — he won't go and get himself into trouble, will he? Then they'll lock him up. Listen, go and see, run after them, please! He'll kill him —"

"No, he won't. He's a sensible man. And besides, he doesn't know that Solem has done you any harm, does he?"

She looks up at me, "Are you asking for yourself?"

"What do you — ?"

"I mean, are you asking for yourself? Sometimes it seems like you're trying to sound me out. *No*, I haven't told my husband this. And now you can think what you want about my honesty. But I have said something, a little, that the man wouldn't leave me alone. He has been here before, he was the one Petra wanted to put up and I wouldn't have in the house. I told Nikolai, 'That man cannot stay here!' And then I told him a little more. But I didn't tell Nikolai anything about myself; so what do you think of my honesty? For that matter, I won't say anything to Nikolai now either, I'll *never* tell him. Why? I don't really owe you any explanation. But I don't mind telling you — yes, let me tell you, please! You see, if I told Nikolai, I wouldn't worry about his rage but about his forgiveness, afraid that we would go on living just as if nothing had happened. He would certainly forgive me, that's his nature; he's fond of me too, and he's a peasant, and, you know, peasants aren't very particular about such things. But he would be a coward if he forgave me, and I don't want him to be a coward, God knows I don't, I'd rather be one myself. I guess we both have to bear with each other in some things, we need to keep what's left. We don't want to be just animals, we want to be human beings, I'm thinking of the future and of our children. . . . Anyway, you shouldn't stand there trying to get me to talk. Why did you ask about it?"

"I only thought that if Nikolai didn't know anything, it wouldn't occur to him to kill the man, as you feared. I wanted to reassure you."

"Yes, you're always so clever, you turn me inside out. I'm sorry I told you, sorry I let you know, I should have kept it to myself till my dying day. Now you'll only think I'm terribly dishonest."

"On the contrary."

"What? I'm not?"

"On the contrary. What you said was quite right, as right as could be. And it was so beautiful."

"God bless you!" she said, sobbing again.

"No, you mustn't cry. Look, here comes Nikolai

strolling up the road, nice and quiet as ever."

"He does? Good. You see, I don't have to bear with him in anything, I spoke hastily. In fact, even if I stopped to think I couldn't find anything. Of course, he uses a few words — I mean, he says a few words differently; but it was her, his sister, who started that. Now I really must go out to meet him."

She started looking for something to put on, it took some time, she was still so jittery; before she was ready Nikolai lumbered into the yard.

"Is that you? You didn't do anything wrong, did you?"

Nikolai's expression is still somewhat stiff, and he answers, "I just took him over to his son."

"Solem has a son here?" I ask.

No one answers. Nikolai goes back to his work, his wife follows him out to the field.

Suddenly it strikes me: Sophie's child!

And I remember very well a day at the Tore Peaks when Sophie came in and reported the latest news about Solem: about the rag on his finger and the finger he never had time to cut off, the ruffian! They got to know each other at that time; later they had probably met in town — Solem was everywhere.

Oh, those women at the Tore Peak resort! Solem was no angel, but he certainly didn't get any better because of them. And then he ran into this poor little creature who had learned only to be a school-mistress. . . .

*

I ought to have realized it before: I don't understand anything anymore.

Something has happened to me.

By chance it finally dawned on me that it is mostly for the sake of the money they want to keep me here, my room and board is to pay for the mare. Sure, that's it.

I ought to have suspected it before, but I'm old. I may perhaps add without being misunderstood that the brain withers before the heart. You can see it in any grandparent.

At first I said bravo to my discovery and said, Bravo, Mrs. Ingeborg, you are a ducat once again! But such is human nature, it began to hurt my feelings. I would have much preferred to pay for the mare right away and be gone, oh, I would have been more than willing to do so! But here I wasn't likely to get anywhere: Nikolai would shake his head like it was a fairy tale. Then I figure out that there cannot really be much owing on the mare anymore, maybe nothing, maybe she was paid for. . . .

And Mrs. Ingeborg toils and moils — if only she doesn't overdo it. She seldom sits down, though she's getting bigger and might need it. She makes the beds, cooks, tends the animals, sews, mends, washes. Most of the time a wisp of gray hair hangs down on either side of her face, she's so busy and leaves the hair alone, it's too short to pin up. But she's so pretty and maternal, lovely skin, lovely mouth, the child and her together are pure beauty. Naturally I've helped her with fetching wood and water during this time, but I've added to her work all the same. When I thought about this my ears burned.

How could I have imagined that anyone would hold on to me for my own sake! With those all too many years and all too little spirit! A good thing I finally wised up.

In a way the discovery made it easier for me to break away; when I packed my bag this time I meant it. Though the child, her boy, stuck to me at least and often wanted to be on my arm, because I showed him so many curious things. It was the child's instinct for that wonderful grandpa of his.

At this time one of Mrs. Ingeborg's sisters came, supposedly to help out. So I pack — I'm weighed down by chagrin at myself and pack. I'll go alone to the steamship landing, to spare Nikolai and the mare, and besides I'm going to excuse everybody from fare-wells and handshakes and "so long," mark my words!

All the same I ended up shaking everybody's hands and thanking them for their hospitality. The other way just wasn't right. I stood in the doorway with the bag already on my back, laughing a little, acting swell and saying that, well, I'd better get moving.

"Oh, you're leaving?" Mrs. Ingeborg asks.

"Yes."

"So suddenly?"

"Didn't I mention it yesterday?"

"Yes, but still. Can't Nikolai drive you?"

"No, thanks."

But now I was again a curiosity for the boy; I had a bag on my back and was wearing a getup with very mysterious buttons, so he wanted to come to me. "Well, for a minute — come on then!" But one minute wouldn't do, not just one extra minute either. For now there was that bag, and of course it had to be opened. Then Nikolai came in.

Mrs. Ingeborg says to me, "You seem to think that just because my sister has come — we do have another room, after all. And besides it's summer now, she can sleep in the barn."

"But my dear, I have to sometime — I, too, have things to do, you know."

"All right," Mrs. Ingeborg says, giving up.

Nikolai offered to drive, but when I declined he said nothing more.

They saw me out and watched me go, the boy was on his mother's arm.

At the bend I turned to wave, to the child that is, not to anyone else, only to the child. But there was nobody in the yard anymore.

XXXVIII

It is for you that I have written this.

Why have I written it in such a way? Because my soul screams with boredom before every Christmas at the same books written in the same manner. I even considered writing in dialect, to be truly Norwegian, but when I realized that you still understood the national language, I gave up the dialect, because, for one thing, it was unusable.

But why have I gathered so many different things into one frame? Little friend, one of the world's most famous literary works was written during a plague, on account of the plague, that's my answer. And, little friend, when you have long held aloof from a humanity you know inside out, you can for once allow yourself the vice to speak again, yes, speak; you have lain fallow for so long, your head is full of a thousand speeches. That's my defense.

If I have you figured out, you will smack your lips here and there over my audacity; in particular, there is a nocturnal episode over which you will rub your hands in glee. But to others you will shake your head and say, How could he write things like that! Oh, you simple little soul, go off and decipher this episode by yourself — it cost me something to deliver it up to you.

Maybe you will also be interested in me and want to inquire about my irons. Certainly, I bring you greetings from them. They are the irons of a fifty-year-old, he has no others. But a difference between me and my fellow wanderers is that I admit it: I have no others. I meant to forge them so great and so red, but they are small irons, with a very faint glow. That's the way it is. They will show up amid the Christmas spread along with all the other products of simpleminded diligence. That's the way it is. The only question is whether, in spite of everything, they are any different from the others' nothings. This you cannot judge: you are the new spirit in Norway and the object of my scorn.

One thing you will admit: you haven't wasted your time in "polite society," it's not with the image of "the lady" I have wanted to regale your little upstart heart. I have written about human beings. But beneath what is said runs another speech, like the artery under the skin, a story within the story. I have followed an incipient literary septuagenarian step by step, reporting the process of his dissolution. I should have done this deed before, but I didn't have years enough; I'm beginning it now, directly and indirectly. I should have done it while the country was groping for ever so long in the shadow of superannuated non-talents — instead I'm doing it now, when the world is beginning to bestow upon me gifts that cast a shadow. Sensation, you will say, pursuit of fame! My innocent little friend, I have fame enough for my last twenty years, afterward I shall be dead. And you? May you live long, you deserve it, oh, may you all but outlive me — in the flesh!

I've just read what a man at the pinnacle of culture has said: Experience shows that when culture spreads it grows thin and colorless. That's not the time to cry out against newcomers bringing renaissance. I can accomplish no renaissance, not now, I came too late. In the days when I could do much and wanted to do more, mediocrity was too powerful. I became a colossus with wooden feet, the fate of so many youths. But now, my tiny little friend, look around you: here